THE BOAT TRIP

HEATHER J. FITT

www.bloodhoundbooks.com

Print ISBN: 978-1-5040-8627-1

For my amazing mum and dad
Thank you for telling me I could be whatever I wanted to be, and
meaning it.

PROLOGUE

Although the overhead lights were off, it was far from dark. Definitely not dark enough for any normal person to be able to sleep. Between the bright yellow light flooding through the window in the door, and the faint glow emitting from various monitors, they would have been as well to leave the light on. Add that to the constant buzzing, squeaking and *snoring* and it was a wonder anyone left hospital feeling well and rested.

I tried to adjust my position. I needed to shuffle just a little bit, but the casts on my legs wouldn't allow it. I banged my head back on the pillows in frustration; the soft woomph noise extremely unsatisfying. I had a choice, stay uncomfortable and hope exhaustion carried me to the land of nod anyway. Or press my buzzer and summon Nurse Beelzebub, who was on nights.

Squeezing my eyes shut, I decided to hang on a bit longer. Disturbing Nurse Beelzebub during the night was only worth doing when absolutely necessary. A few days ago I'd asked her how long it would be before I could go sailing again. She'd taken great delight in telling me I'd be stuck here for at least another week.

'And then there's the physiotherapy to consider,' she said gleefully.

What kind of nurse relished the idea of a patient being laid up for so long?

For now, I could only dream about the sun, warm on my face; a fresh breeze filling the sails; just me and a yacht skimming through the water, not another soul in sight. I usually sailed with a crew, but I knew that, for a little while at least, I wanted to be alone. According to my therapist, I needed to forgive myself for a litany of failures. The only way I could think I might be able to do that was solitude and self-reflection. Sailing had always been my happy place. I hoped it still might be; I couldn't wait to get back on the water, despite the abject disaster that was my last voyage.

Delivering the yacht *Duchess* to St Lucia was supposed to solve my problems and mark the start of a new chapter in my life. Get the monkey off my back so to speak. It should have been straightforward: *Duchess* was a dream to sail, I'd crossed the Atlantic plenty of times, and I had a crew with bags of experience. In reality, almost a month of being virtually cut off from civilisation had made everything ten times worse.

The drama started before we'd even left Scotland, before we'd even raised a sail, or pulled on a rope. I'd inadvertently invited on board a woman who broke up the marriage of two other crew members. I should've done something about it then. If I had things might be different now. Nothing was ever resolved using hindsight though, and looking back would do neither me, nor anyone else, any good.

While every captain has things go wrong, especially on a long journey, the heights of failure I achieved while skippering *Duchess* were quite spectacular. As well as inviting a homewrecker on board, I lost two crew members, sailed into a freak storm, ruined two of my closest friendships and missed the delivery deadline because the yacht ended up a crime scene. Oh yes, and I turned my crew into drug smugglers.

I tried to pinpoint the exact moment it had all gone to rat shit, but there were so many moments you could call the 'start'. Some even before I was asked to deliver *Duchess*.

CHAPTER ONE

NOVEMBER – THREE DAYS BEFORE DEPARTURE

'Helen, it's absolutely fucking freezing. Why the hell did I let you persuade me to do this?'

I had been listening to Erin's complaining since the moment she stepped out of her car and I was beginning to wonder myself why I persuaded her to come with me.

Erin and I had been friends for over thirty years. It was the long kind of friendship that meant we were like sisters, and therefore we were allowed to be annoyed with each other on occasion. Even fall out for a while, until we remembered the good stuff and how much we missed each other.

I reminded myself that Erin needed my patience. Not only was she learning new skills in her forties, she'd also survived a living nightmare in the last two years or so, one that I was pretty sure I couldn't have handled as well as she had; she was allowed a pass here and there. I wasn't known for my patience though and it had been a steep learning curve. I'd learned to allow my mind to drift off, tune out, but she was pushing me today.

'For the life of me I cannot understand what possessed me to agree to go sailing, on the actual *sea*, in November – in Scotland.'

I took a deep breath, trying to settle my irritation. To be fair to Erin, the wind *was* whipping around the harbour at Clyde Marina, propelling the rain straight into our faces, and I wasn't happy about it either.

We continued along the floating walkway towards the boat. I knew the way like the back of my hand; I'd spent the last few months testing *Duchess* out before our trip. I needed to be sure the new boat wouldn't let us down when we were stuck hundreds, maybe thousands of miles from any kind of support.

Erin trundled a little hesitantly behind me. After nearly losing her bedding roll over the side she'd realised she required two hands to steady the trolly containing everything she would need for the next month or more. I felt a glimmer of sympathy for her, these trollies only had wheels in the middle, which meant, until you were used to it, you needed all your concentration to stop it tipping forwards or backwards. This concentration did not seem to prevent her from talking though.

'I can't see for this bloody rain!'

However, it was only a glimmer of sympathy and given her constant complaining, I wasn't inclined to lend a hand. Petty perhaps, but it felt like a small victory.

'Seriously? Could you have parked it any further away?'

'Berthed, and it's not long now.' I imagined Erin rolling her eyes at my back. She hadn't fully embraced sailing vocabulary yet; saying it made her feel silly. I hadn't pushed it, once she heard everyone else speaking the same way, she'd soon change her mind.

We passed row after row of neatly berthed boats of all different shapes and sizes. The orderliness of them both pleased and satisfied me. I was a long way from having OCD, but I did like everything to be just so. I was the kind of person who refolded polo shirts properly in Crew and squared off books in Waterstones after other customers had left them messy.

'Here we are,' I said, coming to a stop beside one of the largest sailing yachts.

'How big did you say it was?' Erin had pushed back the hood of her coat and was eyeing *Duchess* sceptically.

'She. And–'

'What?'

'Boats are shes, not its. And she's fifty-six feet long.' In sailing yacht terms, she was a middle-of-the-road boat, but a beauty nonetheless. I couldn't wait for it to be me, her and the crew, with nothing to do but sail for weeks.

'Oh, right. And how many of us are going?'

'Don't worry, there's plenty of room for all ten of us.'

Erin did not look convinced. I watched as she closed her eyes and took some deep breaths. I waited for her to open them again, recognising her coping mechanism. It was a technique her therapist had taught her to employ when she was feeling overwhelmed and I'd seen it put to good use many times.

I closed my eyes for a moment too. The wind and rain buffeted me, and the floating pontoon wobbled beneath my feet. It felt like home.

But a wet home.

I opened my eyes. The rain wasn't getting any lighter and even though we were wearing foul-weather gear, I wanted to avoid getting any colder or wetter.

'Come on. Let's get your stuff on board and then we can dry off a bit and I'll give you the tour.'

'Right.' Erin looked back and forth between her belongings and the wire guard ropes. It was a look I'd seen from newbie sailors before; there really was no easy way to transfer things onto a yacht; it took teamwork.

'I'll get on board, you pass everything to me and then we'll take it down below.'

Twenty minutes later Erin and I, and all her stuff, were

standing in the saloon below deck, water dripping from us. We stripped off our outer layers and I stowed them in one of the heads to dry off.

As I closed the door, I turned to see Erin taking everything in. I tried to look at it through her eyes. Newbies had said so many times how the inside of a yacht was somehow both bigger and smaller than it appeared from the outside; a little bit *Alice in Wonderland*. There was also a *lot* of wood.

'I see the sailing business is doing its bit to tackle deforestation. Aren't pine trees endangered or something?'

I shrugged. 'No idea. Let's make a brew. I'll give you the tour while the kettle's boiling.'

I showed Erin the two rear double cabins, which were quite spacious, followed by the tiny bunk-bed cabin on the port side.

'I'm not sleeping in there, am I?' There was genuine fear on Erin's face and I didn't blame her. Although there were two single beds behind the door, one above the other, that was all there was.

'No, we're in one of the fore-cabins. I'll show you.'

Also on the port side was a large U-shaped seating area with extremely impractical white leather cushions. There would be murders if anyone damaged them and I was forced to pay for replacements.

On the opposite side was the chart table – which I'd already covered in charts, pencils, a ruler and my pair of compasses – and a well-equipped galley in front of it.

'We're in here,' I said, opening the port-side cabin door. Inside there was a smallish double bed and lots of clever storage.

'Okay...' Erin drew out the word. 'It's... cosy.'

My patience was at breaking point and I couldn't be trusted to listen to her complain about one more thing.

'Why don't you unpack and make the bed? The others will be arriving soon and we can give them a hand with their stuff. I'll make that brew. Coffee?'

Erin groaned. 'I'd rather have a G&T?'

I quirked an eyebrow, but said nothing. Erin had been turning to alcohol to numb the pain a little too often recently in my opinion. Had it been me, I'm sure I'd be a fully paid-up alcoholic by now, but that wasn't the point and as her friend, I was ready to be the intervention before it became crucial. I thought I'd made it clear alcohol would be minimal on board and definitely *not* while we were actually sailing.

Erin rolled her eyes. 'Fine. Which side do you prefer?'

'Doesn't matter to me. Just make sure everything is put away apart from bedding. You don't want things flying all over the place when it gets rough.'

Seeing Erin's face and before she could start whining about rough seas, I handed her the sheet and suggested she make sure it was tucked in tight.

I took my time making our drinks, allowing myself the space to reset. It wouldn't be long before the rest of the crew started to arrive and there would be more distraction – for us both.

'Coffee's ready!'

Erin emerged from our cabin and picked up her cup, peering out of the porthole. 'It looks like the rain has stopped.'

'Hopefully it'll stay off now.'

Erin sat on the sofa, her head tipped back and eyes closed.

'You okay?' I softened into friend-Helen, remembering skipper-Helen could be a bit rigid at times.

'I was just wondering what Rhea would make of all this. Would she laugh at me? Or would she say, *good for you, Mum?*'

I smiled sympathetically and gave myself a moment to search for the right thing to say. I'd run out of platitudes long ago and I was also certain Erin was sick of hearing them.

'I think she would say, *good for you.*'

Erin scoffed just as a voice called from the walkway outside. 'Hello! Anyone there?'

'Coming!' I shouted up the stairs, before turning back to Erin. 'Come on, time to meet some of your crewmates.' I scrambled up the stairs to the deck, leaving Erin to collect herself and follow when she was ready.

Hugo Marshall and Sean Ramsey were standing alongside, smiling and dressed in the now redundant, foul-weather gear. Beside them were two overflowing trolleys, similar to the one Erin and I had just unloaded.

'Hello,' I called and they both waved in reply.

'How's it going?' asked Hugo.

'Good! This is Erin,' I said as she appeared next to me.

'Hi, I'm Sean and this is Hugo,' said the older of the two.

'Right, let's get your stuff on board then. You two are sharing the aft-port cabin,' I said after we'd finished the introductions.

Hugo was one of three experienced sailors, along with me and one of my sons, Connor. The others all had varying degrees of experience, but unlike Hugo and Connor, they were all paying me for the privilege of sailing across the Atlantic. Amateur, but enthusiastic crew were a good way of keeping costs down.

Hugo sprang into action, climbing over the gunwales.

'Why don't you go downstairs and I'll pass things down to you?' Hugo suggested to Erin with a grin. 'If you dump all the stuff in our cabin, we'll sort it out from there.'

Loading the boat with four people sped things up considerably and just when we were about finished, three more crew members arrived on the walkway beside *Duchess*.

Once a married couple, and now divorced, Jonty and Flick had only both been allowed to crew after they had promised faithfully that there would be no arguing. For as long as I'd known Flick she had been desperate to crew a boat across the Atlantic. Over the years, between the children, illness and a lack of space, she'd never quite managed it. I'd made a promise to her last year she'd be first on the list next time and she had vowed to leave the children with Jonty, but he'd ended up passing them on to his parents.

Bringing a divorced couple along was a little perilous, and by God they could fly for one another if the fancy took them, but their money was as good as anyone's.

I smiled fondly at the young man standing beside them. My son, Connor, had crewed with me many times over the years and loved sailing just as much as I did. I wanted nothing more than to wrap Connor up in a big hug, but he hated physical affection, so I shoved my hands into my pockets.

Erin had clearly forgotten, because as soon as she saw him, she scrambled down from the boat and practically threw herself at him. 'Connor!'

Connor managed to disentangle himself without resorting to physically shoving her away. Thankfully Erin was introducing herself to Flick and Jonty instead of paying attention to the grimace on Connor's face. The arrival of people, new people, appeared to have chased away her darkness.

'Hi, I'm Erin, the non-sailor.'

I rolled my eyes. I'd explained to Erin that the crew would be made up of three experienced sailors, while everyone else would have limited experience, with her being the only non-sailor on board. Had I known she would be constantly introducing herself as 'the non-sailor' I wouldn't have said as much.

'Hello.' Jonty was a rather dashing man, something of a George Clooney type with a short, well-groomed beard and a charming smile. 'I'm Jonty and this is Felicity, Flick. If you're the non-sailor, I suppose you'd call us the divorced-less-experienced-sailors.'

'Ignore him,' Felicity said, nudging him out of the way and offering her hand to Erin. 'Please do call me Flick.'

I could see Erin trying to work it out, and so, apparently, could Flick.

'Yes, there is an age gap and no, I don't know what I was thinking either.'

I glossed over any awkwardness and suggested we continue loading belongings in case the rain started again.

The yacht was beginning to feel rather full and everyone seemed to be in good spirits, if not, excitable. Nothing was too much trouble for anyone and there was lots of, 'Oops, sorrys' and 'Here, let me help yous'. I could feel the buzz of being part of a team building inside me. Here I was in my element and the only thing to surpass it would be when we were days away from land with nothing but an expansive ocean around us for thousands of miles.

Nick, who would be sharing with Jonty, had also arrived. Nick was a hugger. Despite that, he avoided Connor, shaking his hand instead and left Erin until last. She looked a little flustered when he pulled her into an embrace. I smothered a smile. Nick was one of my best friends, but I had eyes; he was an attractive man.

'You must be Erin?' Nick said as he wrapped his long arms around Erin's shoulders, pulling her to him. 'Don't worry, we'll look after you. Am I the last?' He looked around the cabin. 'Are we waiting for anyone else?'

'We are. Just–'

'Afternoon, fuckers.' A man was crouched down in the hatch space with an inane grin on his face.

Groans erupted from everyone except Erin and I was certain I heard Flick mutter, 'You've got to be fucking kidding me.'

I had hoped to break the news to everyone gently; too late for that now.

'Who is it?' Erin whispered to me.

Before I had a chance to answer, Flick said, 'That is our very own personal Jonah. He's also a creep, otherwise known as Carl.'

'Seriously, Helen? Jonah?' Hugo said, glaring at me.

'Oh, get over it. There are no silly superstitions on my boats and as annoying as he may be, his money is as good as anyone's, plus he has more experience than most of you. How about we skip the theatrics and whingeing, and get his stuff stowed.' I turned back to my charts, leaving them to get on with it.

'Jonah?' I heard Erin question Flick.

'Yeah, Jonah, the Bible story. Look it up. Bad shit happened when Jonah was on board and bad shit *always* happens when Carl's on board.'

CHAPTER TWO

NOVEMBER – TWO DAYS BEFORE DEPARTURE

I suggested we spent the evening eating and entertaining ourselves on board. It was framed as a suggestion, but really I was adamant. It was important for us all to get to know each other, and become comfortable with each other as quickly as possible.

Of course what I really meant was, I wanted Erin to get to know everyone else – the rest of them had all sailed with one another at some point.

'Our final crew member will be arriving tomorrow, so I think we'll leave watches and rotas and all that stuff until then. There's no point in me going over it twice,' I announced while we were all settled around the table for dinner.

'Who is it? Anyone we know?' Jonty asked.

'I don't think so.' I shook my head. 'She's from the east coast, her name's Arabella.'

Jonty frowned, but said no more and continued eating.

'Carl and Connor, you two are on washing-up duty tonight.' I glanced in their direction.

'Okay.' Connor stood up and started collecting dishes from those who had finished.

'What? Why me?' Carl sounded like a whiney tweenager being asked to clean their bedroom.

'Because you were last on board. Everyone else has either helped load, or cooked your meal. And because I said so.' I used my sharpest tongue. I needed everyone to understand immediately that I was the skipper. The sooner they got that, the better; I couldn't have people arguing with me, or questioning me when their safety might be at risk.

'So just because I wasn't here earlier, I'm being punished?'

'Stop being a dick, Carl,' said Sean. 'You're not being punished. We follow the skipper's orders, you know that. Tomorrow it'll be someone else's turn.' Sean's reply brooked no nonsense and as grateful as I was to him for having my back, it was also annoying. Carl should have just accepted what I said the first time.

'I don't expect to have my orders questioned, Carl. Whether that's me telling you to clean the heads, or me telling you what to do in an emergency. Clear?'

After an incredible amount of grumbling from a man in his mid-thirties, Carl helped Connor clear the table, and together they began washing, drying and putting away the dishes.

Once the excessive clattering and huffing had finished, the saloon settled into an easy and relaxed atmosphere. Felicity, Sean and I gathered around the chart table, chatting quietly, while Hugo, Jonty and Nick played a card game.

Connor curled into a corner and began to read a well-worn copy of *Jamaica Inn*. Daphne du Maurier was one of his favourite authors. I never understood where he got it from. I liked to read, but I found the classics to be too much. Connor, on the other hand, said he preferred them.

Erin disappeared into our cabin and returned a few moments later with a notebook in her hand. She smiled at me sheepishly and gave a small shrug. I knew her counsellor had suggested she use her writing as therapy and I was pleased to see she was taking it seriously. She'd also spoken of blogging about her experience on *Duchess* and I wondered briefly if she was writing about us. She sat down at the table, and after a few moments of staring into space, she opened the notebook and began writing.

I turned my attention back to Flick and Sean, we were discussing why there was really only one route we could take travelling east to west.

For the next little while, everything was peaceful, until, 'No, you can't!'

'What's going on?' I gently pressed Flick out of the way.

'Nothing. I'm going for a walk.' Carl, red-faced, stomped up on the stairs and out into the blustery evening.

'What happened?' I asked Erin.

'He wanted to see what I was writing.'

I pressed my lips together to prevent me from saying what instinctively came to mind. Instead, I said, 'I'll have a word with him.'

'No... don't. I don't want any hassle.' Then, 'Is he always like that?' Erin was asking the room generally.

'Most of the time. He usually calms down once we're sailing.' The others murmured their assent.

Everyone went back to their activities, but I kept my eye on Erin. She was pale-faced and, perched on the edge of the seat, looked like she wanted to run away. I knew my friend, and the altercation had upset her more than she was willing to admit to a room full of strangers.

A short while later I noticed Erin slip into our cabin. It was early yet, but with Carl being outside somewhere, I understood her bed was the only place she could escape to.

The next morning I was woken by a clattering noise and when I looked, there was a space in the bed beside me.

'Ssh!'

'For fuck sake...'

Voices came from the other cabins. Noises carried on board and sailors valued their sleep.

'Sorry,' I heard Erin stage-whisper in response.

She'd get used to it – either that, or she'd face the wrath of her crewmates. I didn't need to be up yet, so I rolled over and closed my eyes. I allowed the gentle rocking of the boat to lull me into a half sleep.

I managed to doze for half an hour or so before I gave up.

I slipped on a pair of jogging bottoms and a sweatshirt over my PJs and crept as quietly as I could into the galley. Erin had fallen asleep on the sofa, a full mug of coffee on the table in front of her. Her head was tipped back and resting on the top of the cushion, her mouth hanging open. I stifled a giggle. Why didn't I have my phone on me?

I made my coffee and padded quietly over to the sofa, *Duchess* had other ideas and creaked in alarm.

Erin's eyes flew open and she sat bolt upright, looking around wildly.

'Sorry, I didn't mean to wake you,' I whispered.

''S okay, I forgot where I was. Thought I was at home and there was someone in my bedroom.' She took a sip of her coffee and grimaced. Cold, I guessed.

'Could you not sleep?'

'No.' Erin rubbed her face. 'I woke up every time I needed to roll over. And the noise! Dear God, why didn't you warn me about the noise?'

'I don't hear it anymore, so I forget it's there.' I shrugged. 'You'll get used to it soon enough. You'll learn to rest when you can; crewing a boat across the Atlantic is physically and mentally exhausting and you need to be prepared for that.'

'I know, you said.' Erin stared into her cup. 'What *is* that noise by the way? And you never mentioned it feeling like you were sleeping on a see-saw.'

'Ha! I hate to break it to you, but the see-saw thing is only going to get worse. The marina is basically a mill pond compared to the open sea. As for the noises, the tapping noise is the halyards hitting the masts and the slapping noise is the water lapping the side of the boat.'

Erin groaned.

This was a brand-new boat and I'd spent the last four and a half months testing her and resolving everything on the snagging list, so there shouldn't need to be any repairs. But, this was still a relatively new boat, so everything needed to be double-checked to make sure it was in working order. Breaking down halfway across the Atlantic with nothing but a sat phone for communication was not something I wanted to have to consider. We also needed to check we had enough food and water to make it to Gran Canaria, which would hopefully only take ten to twelve days. I was certain we had plenty, but my brain wouldn't let me be until I had confirmed it.

Erin cleared her throat. 'So, what's the plan for today?'

I gave her a quick rundown. 'We'll also fill up the fuel tank, but ideally, we want to sail the whole way and conserve as much fuel as possible.'

'Why might we not sail all the way?'

'If the wind suddenly drops, or changes direction it can make things difficult. It shouldn't be a problem at this time of year. Although we can make reasonable predictions, Mother Nature is a law unto herself.'

Erin paled slightly.

I wanted us all to have an early night too. We needed to leave as soon as the sun was up the following morning to catch the tide and begin our journey.

By now, the rest of the crew had started to appear, most looking bleary eyed. I asked Nick to help me prepare breakfast, and make coffee for everyone. Before long we were all sat round the table, idly chatting.

'Once we've finished breakfast, Erin, I'll give you a tour of the deck.'

'I can do that if you want?' Hugo had a mouth full of sausage sandwich as he spoke.

'No, that's okay, I'll do it.' If I showed Erin round and missed something, then I could only blame myself.

Hugo waved his food in the air in a gesture of agreement, choosing not to spray crumbs all over everyone this time.

It was cold on deck, but thankfully, the wind had blown the rain clouds out to sea and it was dry. We started in the cockpit.

'Why does it have two steering wheels?'

'Sometimes when we're sailing we can tip over a bit to either side, depending on the wind. It's called heeling over. When that happens the main sail and the head sail would obscure the driver's view if there was only one steering wheel in the middle. Having two like this means whoever is steering the boat can stand on the high side and see where we are going.'

'Okay...' Judging by the look on Erin's face, she did not share my love of heeling. Maybe she'd feel differently once she'd experienced the exhilaration and freedom it brought. Maybe.

'These are the instruments we use when we're at the helm. You have a chart plotter, an auto-pilot and this one shows us the depth underneath us, our speed, the wind and things like that.' I glanced at Erin who looked like she'd just seen the Kraken climbing over the side of the boat. 'Don't worry,' I said with a laugh, 'you won't be here alone and no one is expecting you to know how to use them. You'll pick up some of it as you go and don't be afraid to ask questions.'

'Okay, what's next?'

Erin's lack of curiosity was a little surprising; she was a writer after all, but I suppose we had covered some of this on her training sails earlier in the year. We moved on to the ropes, or lines as we called them on board and I was certain she was utterly confused when I tried to explain some were also called sheets, but only if they controlled a sail.

Erin spent some time asking me to repeat myself. Her entire life was made up of words and vocabulary and for as long as I'd known her, she'd prided herself on getting it right. Maybe she was becoming more comfortable with our sailing vernacular.

'What's down there?' Erin was pointing at a skylight fitted into the deck near *Duchess*'s bow.

'It's the skipper's cabin. Here, look.' I bent down and unlocked the skylight, before pulling it open. I jumped down inside and beckoned Erin to follow me.

'Boats like this are often chartered by groups of people who don't have a lot of experience, so they hire a skipper along with the yacht and, if there isn't room in the main cabin, this is where the skipper sleeps.'

Erin looked around at the tiny space. There was a small single bed, and a head and not a lot else. It wasn't much bigger than the bunk-bed cabin in the saloon.

Finally, Erin looked up. 'Is this the only way in and out? Though the skylight?'

'Yep.' I nodded, waiting for her reaction.

'Fuck that. I wouldn't sleep down here for love nor money.'

I laughed: her reaction was no different to most people's. It wasn't my favourite place to sleep, but it was a bed, and if you were skippering a bunch of idiots, then it was wonderfully private too.

We returned below deck and Hugo offered to go over some of the more common knots we would need to use with Erin. Flick and Sean joined in too and before I knew it, they were all reciting the rhyme we learned to remember about how to tie a bowline.

Jonty and I listened in amusement while we prepared lunch.

'The rabbit comes up through the burrow, around the tree, back down the burrow. And away goes he.'

'What?' Erin's face was a picture of frustration.

'Is he teaching you about the rabbit?' Connor asked as he came down the stairs.

'Yeah, but even that doesn't make sense.'

'It will, just stick with it. Before you know it, you'll be able to tie one with your eyes closed.' Connor grabbed a piece of rope, closed his eyes and tied the perfect bowline. I grinned; watching my son's party trick never got old.

The others, not to be outdone, and with renewed determination began reciting the poem under their breaths, tying and untying their pieces of rope. By the time lunch was ready, they'd all nailed it.

CHAPTER THREE

NOVEMBER – ONE DAY BEFORE DEPARTURE

When I woke on the second morning, the bed beside me was deserted again. I sighed. Crewing a boat on a long-haul sail was amongst the most tiring things I had ever experienced, and I found it easy to sleep on board. Erin had barely sailed around the marina before and wasn't exactly the fittest of people anyway. Unless she found a way to sleep when she could, she was going to find the journey hellish.

With the exception of Erin, who was sitting in her usual spot with her Kindle to one side and scribbling in a notebook, I was first up. It was how I liked it. When I first started sailing, I'd crewed with some lazy skippers and I vowed I would never be like them.

'How long have you been up?' I asked, placing a hot coffee beside her.

'Only about an hour. And before you say anything,' Erin held her hand up, 'I know I need to find a way to sleep, but I can't right now.'

I decided to side-step the argument. 'What are you writing about?' I nodded towards her notebook, which she closed quickly.

'A few different things. I've had a bit of an idea for a book and I'm trying to write down my feelings about Rhea. Sometimes they're so overwhelming, you know?'

I didn't know, but I nodded anyway. 'Is it helping?'

She thought for a few moments, staring at the light coming through the porthole opposite. 'I suppose you could say it's giving me some... understanding. About how I feel. There's no one judging what I write in here, so I can be totally honest. It's one of the reasons I don't want anyone else reading it.'

I thought back to the first night when Erin had snapped at Carl and it kind of made sense now.

Soon after, we could hear movement from the cabins. Erin closed her notebook and slid it under her Kindle, which she then turned on and began to read. I somehow understood her need for solitude when it came to thinking about Rhea. Although no one could hear her thoughts, I guess she felt vulnerable having them in the presence of strangers.

We ate a light breakfast, and as people became both caffeinated and satiated, the conversation flowed. I allowed myself a small moment of pride at having collected together a group of people who gelled so quickly. Even Carl wasn't being his usual dickish self.

After we'd eaten, Erin asked me to show her the charts and how I worked out how we were going to get to Gran Canaria.

'You're in for it now.' Nick laughed.

'What do you mean?'

'Nothing, just don't say I didn't warn you.'

'I'm not that bad!' But I did regard Erin sceptically for a moment before agreeing.

After explaining the process in great detail, I caught Erin and Nick grinning and rolling their eyes at one another. Okay, so maybe I got lost in the explanation, but charting courses is one of my favourite things about sailing and if you asked me about it, well, that was your own fault.

'Why don't you try?' I said, handing Erin a pencil and a ruler.

She took them from me slightly reluctantly and just as she was preparing to draw her first line we heard footsteps, and felt someone walking along the pontoon. Feeling the boat wobble as someone walks by takes a bit of getting used to, but it's a handy sort of doorbell.

A moment later the boat dipped as someone climbed on board and I could hear faint conversation. 'Must be Arabella.'

Sean came down first, closely followed by a new set of feet. The look on his face surprised me. Gone were the constant smile and cheeky twinkle. They'd been replaced instead by something I could only describe as shock.

'Arabella's here.' Sean spoke softly, but with an edge I wasn't used to.

'Bella's fine actually. You must be Helen?'

The woman he came down the stairs with had long dark hair, which was pulled up into a ponytail. She also looked like she was in need of a good meal: there couldn't have been an ounce of fat on her. There was something Italian-looking about her, but I couldn't for the life of me tell you why I thought that.

'Yes, good to have you on board.' I shook Bella's outstretched hand.

'Bella?' Jonty had come out of his cabin and wore a similar look to Sean.

'Oh, hey Jonty.'

'You two know each other?'

'Sort of.' Jonty jumped in quickly as Bella opened her mouth to speak.

She regarded him in silence for a moment before saying, 'Yeah, sort of.'

Odd. There was something weird going on here, but no one was elaborating. I switched my eyes back and forth between them looking for some kind of clue as to why an awkward atmosphere had descended. They were giving me nothing.

'Okay,' I said, clapping my hands, 'let's get your stuff on board and stowed and then we'll have some lunch. After that we'll talk duties, watches and partners.'

Erin volunteered to make lunch; I was certain she was trying to keep busy. What was she avoiding? A volunteer was better than a conscript though, so I let her crack on. The others went to help Bella with her things.

'That was a bit odd,' Erin said once we were alone.

'What was?'

'Didn't you see Sean's face? And it was clear Jonty and Bella knew each other more than "sort of".'

'Do you think? I'll speak to Sean later, make sure he's all right,' I said, playing it down. Erin's writer brain often went into overdrive, but on this occasion I thought she might've been right.

'What the fuck are you doing here?' The yell came from outside. Erin and I exchanged looks and hurried up the stairs.

From the deck we could see Flick, hands on hips, glaring at Bella. Flick looked like she was ready to pounce on her prey at any moment, but rather than shrinking back, Bella just put her hands in her pockets and smirked.

'I'm part of the crew, in fact, I believe we're sharing a bunk. Isn't that right, Helen?'

'The fuck we are,' Flick replied before I could speak. 'I am not sharing with her, no fucking chance. In fact, I'm not going at all if she's going.'

Oh for fuck sake.

By now the rest of the crew had stopped what they were doing and were watching the scene before them.

'Felicity, please lower your voice and stop swea–'

'Don't. You. Dare,' Flick growled, cutting Jonty off before he could finish.

Bella was still smirking and Flick looked like she was ready to punch it from her face.

Jonty and Sean were avoiding eye contact with anyone and

25

the others just looked confused and perhaps even a little amused. The marina wasn't busy: it was too cold for most sailors in November, but I could still see a few nosey-parkers watching from nearby boats.

I waited, wondering who would speak first. What the hell was going on here? Erin's eyes had taken on a sparkle I hadn't seen from her since before Rhea. She was enjoying this and a memory of a previous conversation nudged me. Something about conflict making a story.

It was desperately cold and no one was giving an inch. I put on my best skipper's voice. 'Why don't we get Bella's stuff on board, and then we can all have a chat?'

'No, I'm going for a walk.' Flick turned and stalked off up the pontoon. 'And I meant what I said, if she's going I'm not,' she called back over her shoulder.

We could crew the boat without Flick. She wasn't one of the experienced sailors, but I knew how desperate she was to crew a yacht to the Caribbean. She'd also already paid her way, and I couldn't give her back the money.

'I'll go after her,' Jonty said quietly.

I wasn't sure that was the best idea, but he knew her better than anyone else. And, I was now in no doubt he knew what the problem was too.

'Right!' I clapped my hands. 'Everyone back to whatever they were doing. Show's over. Carl, Sean, you two help Bella. Erin, how's that lunch coming along?'

Everyone scrambled back to their duties and I followed Erin back down below. I resumed my usual seat behind the chart table, but the maps had lost my interest and instead I thought over everything I'd just seen and heard. Flick was normally so even-tempered, not at all like most of the new-money, married-rich, wannabe-yachties I was used to. Bella must've done something to *really* piss her off.

'That was a bit... dramatic.'

'Hmm?' I pulled my eyes away from the view out the porthole.

'Flick, screaming at Bella like that.'

'Oh, yeah, I suppose it was.'

'Did you know they knew each other?' It was obvious now: Erin was digging.

'No. I mean, I wouldn't have been surprised if they did know each other, or at least know *of* each other. Bella found out about the crossing through a friend, so...' I shrugged. 'But no, I didn't know Flick absolutely hates her, or she would never have been welcome.'

'I wonder what happened.'

'I don't know, and to be honest I don't really care either. They've both paid their way though. I suppose I should go and talk to Flick.' I blew out a frustrated breath.

Bella trotted down the stairs, a small backpack in one hand. 'Which is my bunk?'

I stared at her for a moment, thinking before I spoke. Bella had been right when she had said she and Flick were supposed to share a bunk, but there was no way that could happen, even if I did manage to change Flick's mind.

'I think, after the scene I just witnessed, it's best if we have a swap round actually. I'll move my things and share with Flick. Bella, you can bunk with Erin. I hope that's okay with you, Erin.'

Without waiting for an answer, I turned and walked to our cabin. Erin would just have to deal with it.

Behind me, the two women were chatting, awkwardly.

'Sorry about that,' Bella said.

'It's fine, I'm sure it'll be fun.' There was little enthusiasm in Erin's voice.

After stuffing my things into my bag, I stepped back into the saloon and opened the other fore-cabin door, dumping the bag on the bed. 'I'll sort that later.'

Erin turned to Bella. 'I'm sleeping on the left as you look at the bed. I hope that's okay?'

'Sure, no problem. I can sleep anywhere,' she said with a shrug.

'I'll leave you two to get to know one another. Bella, could you help Erin finish lunch? I'm going to find Flick and Jonty.'

CHAPTER FOUR

NOVEMBER – AFTERNOON BEFORE DEPARTURE

I eventually found Flick and Jonty shouting at each other outside the shower block. Actually, Jonty was trying to shout, but every time he opened his mouth to speak Flick cut him off.

'Don't give me your bullshit, Jonty. You had to have known.'

'You keep saying that, but–'

'Helen even told you her name!'

Jonty turned and stamped away a few steps, his fingers tugging at his hair. He stopped as soon as he saw me walking up the pontoon. Turning back towards Flick, he spoke to her with a lowered voice and Flick's eyes turned towards me.

'I'm not coming,' Flick shouted over.

Jonty threw his hands up in the air, spinning to face the other way. Dramatic, yes, but everything about Jonty was a bit OTT.

I didn't say anything immediately, just nodded in what I hoped was a thoughtful manner. 'Why don't we go inside, grab a drink and talk about it?'

Flick screwed up her face and before she could fly into another rage, I cut her off. 'No decisions need to be made right now, and I'm not going to force you to do something you don't want to do. But we can at least talk about it.'

'Fine.' Flick folded her arms and stalked off towards the club house.

'You coming?' I asked Jonty.

'Sure.' He sounded defeated. 'For all the good it'll do.' He held out an arm indicating I should go before him.

I took a breath and tried to plan what I was going to say to Flick. The truth of the matter was, I didn't do drama and it didn't matter if Flick came with us or not, other than the money she'd given me to pay her passage was already gone and I couldn't afford to pay her back. By rights, I didn't have to give her a refund anyway, not this close to departure day, but the thought of her asking and me having to refuse made me feel sick. Any kind of discussion around money made me anxious.

But I couldn't say any of that to her, so instead I planned to concentrate on what it would mean for Flick. Everything had been going according to plan – until Bella appeared.

Inside the club house, we found Flick already seated at a table in the corner away from the bar. She needn't have bothered; there was no one around, other than the barman, who was placing a large glass of red wine in front of her. I asked Jonty to get us both a drink, staring at him hard, hoping he would get the message and give me a few minutes alone with Flick.

'I'll just have an orange and lemonade, thanks.' Alcohol agrees with me even less than it does most people, and I couldn't have a hangover tomorrow. I pulled out a chair across from Flick who was staring into her glass. I didn't pull it in; I thought it best to give us both a bit of space.

'Do you want to tell me what's going on?'

'No.'

So that's how it was going to be.

'Okay. How about I speak for a minute? It's clear you don't like Bella, and Jonty has something to do with it. Obviously I don't know for certain what's gone on, but I can take a guess.' Flick glanced up at me then and I held my hand up. 'I don't want to know: your business is your business. What I will say though, is are you really going to let this – let her – ruin your dream? Sure, you could sign on next year, but what's to say something else doesn't come along and spoil it? The same as it has every other year so far.'

Her head still down, she stared hard at me through her eyelashes. I had her attention now. I could almost see her brain churning through the points I'd made.

'Here you go. No ice, sorry,' Jonty said as he placed my drink in front of me. He looked first at Flick and then at me, questions written all over his face. I shrugged and shook my head, the ball was in Flick's court.

'What's been said?' Jonty wasn't known for his patience any more than I was, so I repeated more or less what I'd said in his absence. 'Helen's right you know, it might be years before you get another opportunity.'

'Oh what do you care? You couldn't give two shits whether I go or not. You couldn't even handle looking after the kids on your own; instead you had to persuade your parents to take them and hire a nanny!'

I sat back and let them argue. Maybe this was something that had to be released into the atmosphere for them both to move on. Once we started going round in circles though, I stepped in.

'You're just repeating yourselves now. It's decision time. I can't sit here all day; I need to get back to *Duchess* and brief the rest of the crew. Flick, what are you doing?' I held my breath.

'You're right, Helen, I really do want to crew *Duchess*, but...' She closed her eyes and breathed deeply. 'Okay, but I have conditions.'

'For fu–'

'Let her speak, Jonty.'

'I'm not sharing a bunk with her; I'm not doing a watch with her; and I will not be speaking to her unless absolutely necessary.

And by that I mean, the boat is sinking or there is a man overboard situation.'

Jesus, it was like dealing with six-year-olds. 'I think we can accommodate that. I've already switched cabins with Bella, and you two weren't on watch together anyway.'

At last, we made our way back to *Duchess*.

'Can I have everyone in the saloon, please,' I called out once I was back on board. I received plenty of questioning looks, but ignored them, pretending I hadn't seen or didn't understand. I didn't see the point in making some kind of grand announcement. They'd figure it out.

Everyone gathered on the sofa; Flick at one end, Bella at the other. I decided to ignore them unless it impacted on the safety or the harmony of my crew. Their fight was their fight, I wasn't about to insert myself into a situation that I had no way of resolving.

'Right, let's talk watches. I'm partnering everyone up in twos and we'll have the standard watches. If anyone doesn't know what those are, we can talk about it afterwards, but basically, you'll be on watch for no more than four hours at a time with plenty of rest in between. Erin, you're with me and we'll be taking the first sail tomorrow morning. Hugo is with Flick; Connor, you're with Carl; Nick and Jonty, you two are together; and Bella and Sean are the final two.' I knew not everyone would be happy with their partner, but they made the most sense. Connor would forgive me eventually; I partnered him with Carl because I knew he wouldn't make the same kind of fuss the others might, and he knew it too.

'I've written out the rotations. I'll put it up in the galley for your reference. Please remember, when it's your turn for mother watch, you're responsible for cooking, cleaning, making drinks and generally making sure the place is kept tidy. That does *not* mean everyone else can just leave shit lying around though. It doesn't take much for a space this small to end up in a mess.'

I checked the list I'd made, ticking off each item we'd already discussed.

'Allergies and medical conditions. Does anyone have either of those I need to be aware of? Everyone needs to know, so you might as well say now.'

'I have an allergy to cow's milk.' Bella raised her hand to her shoulder.

'Oo, okay. How bad are we talking?'

'I'd go into anaphylactic shock and need my EpiPen.'

'Right! We'll need to keep your EpiPen in the first aid kit then, so everyone knows where to find it – just in case. Can you bring it to me afterwards?'

'Sure, no problem. Does everyone know how to use one?'

'That's a really good point.' I looked around the room to see most people nodding. 'Anyone who's unsure come and see me or Bella and we'll talk you through it. Anyone else?'

'I have high blood pressure and take medication for it.' Jonty spoke from the corner.

I nodded while I made a note on my pad. 'I take it you have enough pills, or whatever it is, for the whole trip? Even if we're delayed?'

'Yep. I've got two months' worth. I don't think there'll be a problem, but thought I should let you know.'

'Thanks, better to be safe than sorry. Is that it?' Another quick glance around the room confirmed everyone was done. 'Does anyone have any questions?' I looked for the tell-tale signs someone was going to complain about something. 'No? Excellent. Well, if you do think of something, please ask. There are no silly questions. Connor and Carl, could you organise our meal tonight, please, since you guys don't have duty tomorrow.'

CHAPTER FIVE

NOVEMBER – DEPARTURE DAY, TAKE TWO

It was departure day take two, and everyone was bright-eyed and bushy-tailed despite the fact we were up early to catch the tide. We should have left the day before, but the weather was so awful I'd had no option but to delay it by twenty-four hours.

I should have known there would an argument about it. Sailors were notoriously superstitious, even in the twenty-first century.

'We can't sail tomorrow!' Carl had been aghast.

I rolled my eyes. We were hunkered down in the saloon waiting for the high winds and rain to die down.

'You're a fine one to talk – Jonah,' Jonty muttered.

'Why not?' Erin asked.

'Because it's bad luck,' Carl replied.

'But why?'

I smiled at that. Erin was as bad as a two-year-old with the 'why' game when she wanted information.

'Because you can't set sail on a Friday – the same day as Christ was crucified – apparently.' Nick's tone was derisory.

'Oh. There are quite a few superstitions about sailing, aren't there?'

'Hundreds and plenty around the Bible too. But – and this is important – they're all nonsense.' I spoke like they were children.

'No, they–'

'Enough! Next you'll be telling me there shouldn't be women on board and if we start whistling it'll bring a storm.' I rolled my eyes. 'Shall I throw the bananas overboard while I'm at it? We sail as we planned to, after high tide, just a day later.'

I had eyed each of them, daring someone to say another word on the subject. Sailing could be dangerous enough as it was without adding irrational unfounded fears into the mix.

I woke with excitement bouncing around in my belly. People will tell you I'm quite a serious person, and they are right, but during the few hours before we set sail on a long journey, I am always giddier than a kid at Christmas.

I didn't have long to savour my usual solitary coffee that morning, but it didn't matter; I enjoyed the buzz of anticipation that came with my crew getting themselves ready.

I was reminded all was not rosy though, when Flick emerged from our cabin with a scowl on her face.

'Coffee?'

'Please.' Her scowl only intensified when Bella squeezed past her on the way to the heads.

'If the wind changes you'll stay like that.' I went for light-hearted, but it fell flat.

'I'm not talking to her.'

I handed her a steaming cup.

'Is this oat milk?'

'Yes. And I'm not asking you to be best mates. Just be civil – for everyone else's sake.'

Flick snorted and slumped onto the sofa.

When we'd got back on board after persuading Flick to sail, I had a private chat with Bella and later that evening confided in Erin. I wasn't one for gossip, but I needed to talk this one out and Erin had always been a confidante. What no one seemed willing to talk about was *why* Flick felt as she did. I could guess at what was going on, but without confirmation I wasn't willing to speculate. Flick had refused point-blank to talk about it and Jonty also remained tight-lipped. It also didn't explain why Sean was giving Bella a wide berth either; it wasn't as if he and Flick were close.

We took advantage of the facilities in the marina and had our last proper shower until we reached Gran Canaria. There was a shower on board, but it was small and since water was in limited supply, we were allowed no longer than five minutes under the spray.

After everyone had eaten it was finally time to cast off, sail down the Firth of Clyde, past the Isle of Arran and out into the Irish Sea.

'Everyone up on deck, please.'

Erin's head popped up, meerkat-like, from where she, yet again, had her nose in her notebook. What was she writing about this time? More about Rhea, and how she felt about it all? Or maybe a diary? Oh God, was she making a permanent record of our private conversation? I pushed the thought away, feeling guilty; Erin knew where the line was.

'What?'

'It's tradition. Everyone starts off each voyage on the deck – together.'

'But I thought "silly superstitions" weren't allowed on your boats?' Erin pressed her lips together hiding a grin, but her eyes gave her away.

'Tradition, not superstition. And you're on watch with me anyway. Let's go.' I wasn't prepared to discuss it, so I turned and made my way up the stairs.

The crew were assembled on deck, I took the helm, Erin standing beside me eventually. Sean and Hugo stood by at the fore and aft lines, ready to let slip. We were all similarly dressed in thick jackets, warm hats and gloves with the ends missing from our thumbs and first fingers – undoing a knot with normal gloves on was virtually impossible.

Despite the tension created by the Flick and Bella thing, and everyone's hatred of Carl, there was an air of excitement amongst the crew. This was it: we were actually going to sail to Gran Canaria. Everyone was smiling and looking out towards the Isle of Arran in the distance.

'Everyone keep your eyes open: you might see a golden eagle.' There was a glint of mischief in Hugo's eyes.

'Are you doing that thing where you tell us we might see something rare and then laugh while we keep our eyes glued to the sky?' Erin asked.

'Would I?' Hugo laughed. 'To be fair, you *might* see one, but you are far more likely to see a kestrel or a sparrowhawk.'

'I'm not sure I would know one if it landed on my head,' Bella said, giggling and earning herself another glare from Flick.

'I'll show you if I see one. We've all to be on deck until we sail out of the firth anyway.'

'Why do we have to do that, again?' Carl asked. I was beginning to regret having him on board at all.

'In my opinion, it makes us more of a team. We set sail together and we tie up together when we arrive.' I kept my eyes on the sea in front of me. Not that I needed to. I'd sailed in and out of the Clyde Firth on this route so many times, I reckoned I could do it on a moonless night with a blindfold on.

'Does it work?' Bella asked.

'It doesn't not work; let's put it that way.'

We lapsed into silence and I watched as the others took in the views around us. Despite the cold and the hard grey sky above us, there was a beauty to the scenery that one could not fully appreciate from the shore. I opened my eyes wider as if that might help me to take more of it in. I hoped I would never get used to the beauty of my homeland.

Although the sea around us was murky slate grey, the sight

before us was as stunning as always. The island was a riot of greens and yellows, with Goatfell, Arran's highest mountain, standing proud in the centre. I turned and saw the Calmac ferry leaving Ardrossan harbour behind us and watched it make its way across the firth towards Brodick. Becoming attuned to the constant motion of the boat was as familiar to me as breathing. I quickly felt the usual calm descend over me as I took a deep breath of salty cold air.

'Hugo and Flick, you'd better get going,' I called to where they were now standing near the bow.

'What are they doing?' Erin asked.

'They're on the first mother watch. It's their job to make everyone's food, and keep the heads and saloon clean. Stuff like that.'

Erin looked at her watch. 'But it's still early.'

'It is, but time can fly by on a boat when you're least expecting it. It's always best to be as organised as you can be. Plus, I really fancy some coffee and cake.'

'Is that a sailing thing, or a Helen thing?'

'Coffee and cake?'

'No, the being as organised as you can.' Erin was taking the piss.

'Both.' I winked at her.

'So, if we fancy a brew, or whatever, we just ask mother watch.'

I side-eyed Erin, trying to figure out if she was serious or not. Her face gave nothing away. 'If you're on watch, it's fine to ask. If you're resting, well, just don't take the piss.'

Twenty minutes later the crew was scattered around *Duchess* drinking hot drinks and munching on cake. A few had gone back down below where it was warm, but Bella, Connor and Nick had stayed on deck to keep us company. I suspected Bella was keeping out of Flick's way.

'Hang on, so first watch *isn't* the first watch of the day? It's actually the last?' We were explaining to Erin what each of the different watches were called and how they were split up across the day.

'Yep. Technically, the first watch of the day, the one directly after midnight, is middle.'

'Okay… and then there are some random two-hour watches in the afternoon weirdly called first and last dog?'

'You're getting it,' Connor said proudly.

We continued to share stories of our previous adventures with Erin, who grew more wide-eyed and incredulous with each one. I let her sit in the cockpit, while I took the wheel. There would be plenty of time for her to learn; it made me happy to see her laughing and smiling with new friends. I was also at my happiest standing peacefully at the helm of a yacht.

Just as we were coming to the end of our watch, and Bella and Sean were preparing to take over, I heard a shout from Bella. She was on the starboard side, the opposite side to the wheel I was steering from.

'What is it?' I shouted above the wind.

I heard heavy footsteps on the wooden stairs as people scrambled up them, racing towards whatever had caused Bella to shout. I scanned the crew I could see. Was there someone missing? A man overboard? Surely not, I would've heard something.

'Look!' Bella was pointing directly at the sea, and for a moment I imagined my worst nightmare. And then I focused and laughed.

At the end of Bella's finger was a pod of dolphins, and they were gliding along beside the boat. Jumping and swimming over each other in a display that felt like it was just for us.

'Oh my goodness, this is wonderful,' Erin exclaimed.

'Just you wait until we're crossing the Atlantic.'

'The bioluminescence has to be seen to be truly appreciated, but it is one of the most beautiful things I have ever seen. And if we're really lucky, we might see a whale.'

Erin's eyes widened. 'I can't wait.'

CHAPTER SIX

NOVEMBER – THE IRISH SEA

We had now been at sea for a little over a day. Erin and I had already done three watches and were now on mother watch. This was the longest and most exhausting stint, but after this we'd be off and there would be plenty of time for resting.

We'd decided to clean the heads and tidy up straight away. It meant we would have the chance for a sit down and a brew before it was time to make lunch. Connor, our unofficial weatherman, was giving us the lowdown for the next twenty-four hours.

'It's all looking good. Not expecting anything that'll cause us any problems between now and when we hit the south coast.'

Despite his reassurances and the fairly calm sail we'd had so far, Erin seemed to look perpetually green. Although I don't think she'd actually been sick, she had been sticking to dry toast and water most of the time. I hoped she found her sea legs soon: the sea was a mill pond in comparison to how it was going to be once we started sailing through the bay.

'Of course, it will get pretty rough once we're past Ireland. Nothing but sea between us and Canada then.'

'Really?' Erin's green face was now tinged with curiosity.

'Really. There's no land to break up the swells, you see. Here, look, I'll show you.' He brought out his phone and loaded Google Maps, pinching and swiping at the screen.

I tried to be positive and hoped Erin wouldn't dwell on what Connor was saying. 'You'll be fine by then. You're just taking a day or two to get used to the motion of the boat – that's totally normal.'

Erin snorted, unconvinced, and took Connor's phone from his outstretched hand. 'Oh wow, you're right. I'd never thought of that before. So when will we get past Ireland?'

Connor squinted at his watch. 'I reckon in about an hour. You should come up top and watch. The way the south coast of Ireland tapers off is unreal, the land slowly disappears until all that's left is the ocean as far as you can see.'

'Will I have time before we need to make lunch?' Erin looked from me to her watch.

'Why don't we make a start now, and then I can finish off?'

'Are you sure?'

'I can't imagine you doing this more than once, so yeah, I'm sure. You don't want to miss it.' I smiled fondly; I wanted her to enjoy the trip and see all the things I often talk about.

'What about you?'

'I've done this journey so many times I've lost count, I don't need to see it again this time round.'

Erin and I got to work in the galley making sandwiches for everyone.

'Oh my God, how did I not realise how difficult this would be?'

Making sandwiches for ten hungry sailors takes a lot longer than you realise.

'Well this isn't quite the same as a quick cheese and ham wrap at home, is it?' Erin said, launching herself after the tub of butter as it slid across the counter-top. I laughed: it was second nature to me, but watching Erin chase after anything she put down was hilarious.

'You've got to find your balance; "ride" the boat.' I demonstrated by exaggerating the bend in my knee and the constant movements I had to make to stay level. All that served to do was earn me a glare from Erin, which made me laugh even more.

'Just have one thing at a time on the side, and then put it away when you're done,' Nick said from where he and Jonty were grinning at the saloon table.

'You better not be laughing at me.' Erin pointed her knife at the men, who roared with laughter as the boat tilted suddenly and Erin staggered like she'd been doing tequila shots all day. I wondered if she might get upset, Erin wasn't always comfortable with people laughing at her, even if there was no malice intended. I needn't have worried though, she saw the funny side and laughed along with them.

Soon after, I sent her to put on her foul-weather gear. I had already begun to feel the swell of the ocean against the hull and we were heeled over quite far already. Erin clambered up the stairs, eager to see the view Connor had promised her.

I finished making lunch, and asked Hugo and Jonty to help me dish it out. I handed up four plates for me and Erin, and the two boys on watch, then climbed the stairs to join them.

The next couple of hours were spent absorbing the scenery around me while the bracing wind stung my face. I was cold but this was my happy place and I wanted to share the whole experience with Erin as much as I could.

'Will it get worse?' Erin called to Connor who was steering. She had to raise her voice to be heard above the wind.

'It's not going to get better, that's for sure,' Carl replied, chuckling. 'We've got the bay to sail past yet and that's rough as fuck.'

'The bay?'

'Yeah, the Bay of Biscay. That bit of France and the top of Spain that curves in.' I drew a semicircle in the air with my finger.

'That'll be a rough twenty-eight hours or so. I'll let you into a little secret, don't put *anything* down unless it's in a cupboard, you *will* lose it,' Connor said.

Erin, who had started to look like she might be enjoying herself, paled a little. There wasn't anything I could do, and there was no point in reassuring her. It *was* going to be rough and she needed to be prepared for it.

I snuggled down into my jacket and laughed along as we regaled Erin with tales of spilled coffee, lost sausage sandwiches, and crewmates throwing up over the side. Funny though the stories were, I hoped Erin heeded the warning wrapped up in our humour. Large swells and a heeled-over sailing boat were things you couldn't train for, not really; I wasn't sure Erin appreciated what was ahead of her.

Eventually, it became too cold to stay on deck and it was almost time to make dinner anyway.

'You coming down?' I asked Erin. 'Get warm before we make dinner?'

'Sure.' Erin made her way to the hatch in front of me.

'Go down backwards and hold on, it's easier when it's like this and we don't need you twisting an ankle or a knee on the way down.'

Later that evening, Hugo and Flick were on watch, Nick, Jonty, Erin and I were sitting around the table in the saloon and everyone else was in bed. Nick and Jonty were on the midnight watch, but after that they had eight straight hours to sleep. I probably should've gone to bed myself, but I was relaxed and enjoying their company.

Conversation eventually came round to Erin's books, as it often did when there were people around she didn't really know. I watched her carefully. She'd struggled to write recently, and I wondered if she'd want to talk about it. I let the conversation go on, ready to step in if Erin looked uncomfortable.

'Would I have heard of anything you've written?' Jonty asked.

'Probably not, I tend to write romance or women's fiction. I can't imagine that's really your thing?'

'Ah, no, chick lit is definitely not my thing.'

Erin bristled and I cringed. If there was one thing Erin hated it was her books being called chick lit. Jonty didn't mean anything by it, so I hoped she'd let it go.

'Didn't you say you were thinking of swapping genres?' I tried to steer the conversation a slightly different way.

'I did.' Erin nodded thoughtfully. 'My agent suggested it. My last few books haven't done that well and we wondered if it was time for a change. That, and it's been… difficult to write happy-ever-after endings recently.' Erin glanced at me. That look told me everything. This was it; she was ready to have the conversation.

'Does that mean you're watching us all and taking notes? Are you going to write a book about sailing to the Caribbean?' Jonty chuckled at his own joke.

'Did you just get sick of writing the happy stuff?' Nick asked.

'No, I, umm…' Erin looked at me again, for reassurance perhaps.

I smiled warmly at her and nodded. *You can do this*, I tried to tell her with my eyes.

'My daughter. She…' Erin cleared her throat and studied the table in front of her. 'She suicided. About two years ago.'

There was no 'about' about it. I knew Erin knew exactly how long ago it had been since Rhea died. Jonty and Nick were as shocked as anybody might be.

'I'm so sorry, Erin. My comment seems so crass now.' Jonty looked mortified.

'It's okay, you weren't to know. And thank you. My therapist says it's good to tell people, if I can. That I shouldn't treat it like some horrible secret. I've found it really tough to talk about, but I'm getting there.' Erin gave me a watery smile.

'You are, and I'm so proud of you.' I squeezed her hand.

Nick reached over the table and held Erin's other hand. 'I'm *so* sorry for your loss. I don't have any other words for you, but I really am sorry.'

Erin gave him the same watery smile she had given me, her eyes filling with tears. She swallowed hard. 'Thanks guys. One day at a time; some days are better than others, and all that stuff.'

Erin found a tissue in her pocket and then wiped her eyes and blew her nose. 'Let's talk about something else.'

'Of course. Whatever you like,' Jonty said.

'Could you maybe answer a question for me? It's something that's been bugging me for a while.'

'I will if I can,' he said, turning his palms upwards.

'What's the deal with Flick and Bella?' Erin lowered her voice.

My eyes widened. That was *not* where I had expected this conversation to go! Had Erin used telling the boys about Rhea's death to garner sympathy so she could ask inappropriate questions? Surely not, but it was such a dramatic change of topic. I caught Sean's look to Jonty. *Well he knows.* Erin and I watched, waiting to see if Jonty would answer.

'It's... I... you should really ask them if you want to know.'

'Oh, of course. Sorry, I shouldn't have asked. I was chatting to Bella about it earlier, but she was called to watch.'

I stared at Erin. I hadn't realised she'd spoken to Bella about it. Why wouldn't she tell me something like that? It made me uncomfortable to think that she'd been asking people about their private lives. Especially when she got so funny about people talking about Rhea. I knew she was a writer, but this felt like too much. Before I could intervene, Jonty spoke.

'Let's just say, we know Bella from a couple of years ago, and there was a falling out. Well, the girls fell out and I was kinda stuck in the middle.'

Erin nodded thoughtfully and offered a small smile. She said nothing and the silence began to feel thick. I should have shut down the whole conversation, but the truth was, I wanted to know too.

Jonty filled the silence. 'To be honest, I had no idea she was a sailor. We met... at a function. I couldn't believe it when I saw her at the marina. Turns out that although she's sailed quite a bit, she's never crossed the Atlantic. So when she heard about this trip through a friend of a friend, it was too good an opportunity for her to let pass and she booked straight away.'

'She came recommended.'

Erin glared at me, why, I wasn't sure.

'Anyway, it's not really something I want to talk about, or should talk about. It's not my story to tell.'

'Oh I'm so sorry Jonty. I didn't mean to pry. I just feel like everyone else knows what's going on except me.'

I narrowed my eyes and raised my eyebrows. Prying was *exactly* what Erin had in mind.

'Well they don't,' Jonty snapped and then said a little more softly, 'Let's just leave it, ay?'

'Who's up for a game of gin rummy?' I took Jonty's hint and pulled out a pack of playing cards, shuffling them furiously.

CHAPTER SEVEN

NOVEMBER – THE BAY OF BISCAY AND NORTHERN SPAIN

Sailing across the Bay of Biscay was bad. Even with thousands of hours logged at sea, and having sailed across the bay more times than I could count, I felt seasick. No one enjoyed that crossing.

The boat and everything in it rocked, swayed and tipped constantly. No one could move more than a step or two without holding onto something, and climbing up and down the stairs between the deck and the saloon was treacherous. Drinks were spilled, plates were held onto and I insisted anyone on deck was strapped on with a lifeline, just in case. As for sleeping, well, let's just say anyone sharing a double became a whole lot closer during the night!

The sea, the boat, the crew and my stomach became a lot calmer once we hit the north of Spain. Knowing now how rough it *could* get, Erin's seasickness abated once we returned to calmer waters. She had quickly become used to the routine on board, and I think she actually started to enjoy it. She mentioned more than once that always having something to do helped the time pass quickly. I didn't really understand anyone wanting time to pass quickly at sea, but she was happy, so I let her be.

The weather was good considering it was wintertime, which meant watches, and the actual sailing of the boat, were relatively straightforward – even for Erin. She'd completed her competent crew course earlier in the summer, which had easily equipped her for this part of the journey at least. Connor kept a close eye on the forecast and would let us know if and when to expect any inclement weather. For the moment though, it looked good all the way to the Canaries.

I spent our watches supervising Erin rather than doing it all myself; there was nothing like practical experience at building confidence. I could see Erin's belief in herself and her abilities increase with every watch. During the day mother watch kept us fed and watered, and when they had nothing else to do, would often stop for a chat. In the evening, when everyone else was in bed and there was nothing to see except the stars, we talked. About old times, about our futures and anything else that came to mind.

We were on the middle watch, or as I liked to call it, the witching hour. It was a sparklingly clear evening, if a little blowy. With no light pollution in the middle of the sea the stars seemed all the brighter. It was freezing cold and we were both wrapped in as many layers as possible. Mother watch had supplied us with flasks of hot drinks to keep us going until we were relieved by Hugo and Flick in four hours' time.

Connor disappeared below deck with a wave, pulling the hatch closed to keep out the cold wind. Erin was staring at his retreating back with an unreadable expression on her face.

'How are you doing?'

Erin turned to me, her eyes flitting over my face as if it might give her the answer. Or at least give her the answer she thought I wanted to hear.

'I mean really. Is it helping? Crewing? Being at sea?'

Her eyes drifted towards the edge of the boat and the sea

beyond. It was a dark night, there wasn't much to see and I wondered what visions were playing out before her.

She was quiet for so long I thought she might not answer. It didn't seem right to push her, so I left her to her thoughts.

'There's no easy way to answer that,' she said eventually with a sigh.

'I didn't imagine there would be, but we have the best part of four hours. If you want to talk, there's time for me to listen.'

'Being here. Being responsible, part of a team, people dependent on you, you have no choice but to be present. To help, get stuck in, do your bit. You know?'

It was a rhetorical question, but I nodded into the darkness anyway, sipping my hot chocolate to stop me from speaking, interrupting her flow.

'It's such a cliché, but I do feel more alive out here. Freer somehow. My imagination has been loosed and I have all these ideas swimming around in my head. Writing down my feelings has made space for them. I write to her, you know. To Rhea. I tell her all about our day and my emotions, both past and present. It all helps, and then out of nowhere I am desperate to speak to her. To actually talk to her and tell her all about this adventure I'm undertaking and it's like finding out she's dead all over again when I remember that I can't.'

Erin was talking about a pain I couldn't even begin to understand. Wasn't it a mother's, a *parent's*, worst nightmare for their child to be taken before them? Danny is not the sort of man I'd hoped he would be. Not the sort of person I thought I'd brought him up to be, but the thought of losing him twisted my stomach.

Thinking about Danny made me grimace, so I thought about Connor instead and felt no guilt. Connor was a lovely young man and everything I'd hoped both my sons would be. He was a joy to spend time with and I knew I could count on him, no matter what. I hoped he knew the same was true for me.

'Honestly, I see such a difference in you already.' I hoped it didn't sound like a platitude; that wasn't how it was intended. It was the truth – Erin was functioning, contributing, which was more than could be said of her a few months ago.

'Really? I wonder if I'll ever get over it sometimes.'

'I don't think you'll ever get over it.'

Erin turned sharply to stare at me.

'I mean it. The death of a child isn't something you're meant to overcome – at least I don't think it is. That doesn't mean you can't live your life. That doesn't mean you have to be in mourning for the rest of your days. I can't imagine what you're going through, have been through, and I never want to. But if it were me, I think I'd want to learn how to make it a part of me. Never forgetting, but not letting it rule me either.'

'Maybe you're right.' Erin stared off into the black sea again and we were quiet for a while. The only sounds were the water slapping against the hull and the wind in our ears. There were no birds, no voices – perhaps the most peaceful place in the world.

'Do you ever worry about Danny?'

It was my turn to look up sharply. No one ever wanted to talk about Danny. He was the elephant in the room. When friends were discussing their families, they would skirt around the fact I had two sons, only ever asking about Connor. It usually helped that he was with me of course; sailing was his life as much as it was mine.

'The honest answer is, I do when I think about him. But I try not to think of him often. It's too much, too hard to get my head around.' I paused and then whispered, 'Sometimes I tell myself I only have one son.' I waited, expecting Erin to tell me off. Shout at me for not appreciating what I had, what she'd lost.

When I looked over at her, she was nodding thoughtfully. 'By the way, I wanted to say, thank you.'

'Thank you for what?' Erin's change of subject had taken me a little by surprise.

'For everything, I suppose. You held me up when I couldn't hold myself up. Buying my shopping, making me eat – making me shower.' We both chuckled at that, remembering when I'd come round after being at sea for a week to find Erin in the same clothes as I'd left her in. She was surrounded by takeaway wrappers and empty wine bottles – it had not been her finest hour.

'It's what friends do.' I reached out and gripped her gloved hand in mine.

'I know, but I also know I was a lot. And now you've brought me along on this trip, and I know I haven't been easy, but I do appreciate it.'

I waved away her self-criticism, but I couldn't bring myself to vocalise any disagreement. She had been a lot, and she hadn't been easy, but agreeing with her seemed like a step too far.

'I don't want to talk about heavy stuff anymore,' Erin said quietly.

We chatted for the rest of our watch, asking each other all sorts of random questions and talking off on tangents; keeping it light and fluffy. We pointed out star formations and Erin gave them silly names; I told her the right ones, all the while trying to spot shooting stars.

'I wonder how many other people in the world are looking at these exact same stars as us?' I asked on a whim.

'Thousands? None?'

I suspected she was right on both counts.

CHAPTER EIGHT

NOVEMBER – PORTUGAL

By the fourth day of our watch rotation I was more than ready for mother watch followed by some downtime. As much as I enjoyed being at the helm, I wanted to relax a bit before we arrived in Gran Canaria.

On the plus side, the weather had improved and jackets were really only required at night, or if the wind was particularly forceful. There was a little glow in my chest and a smile tugged at my lips when I thought about how the weather would only get warmer from now on.

Erin and I had made, eaten and cleared up after lunch. Connor and Carl were on watch, and after taking them drinks and snacks, I sat down at the table with an old sailing magazine. Erin was sitting along the bench from me, writing as usual, and the others were dotted around *Duchess* doing their own thing.

'How's it going?' I asked Erin, nodding towards her laptop.

'What?' She looked up, confused. I never understood how she managed to block everyone and everything out to the point someone talking directly to her came as a surprise.

'Whatever it is you're writing,' I said, waving a hand in her direction, 'how's it going?'

'Oh, fine. Thanks.' Erin dipped her head and I watched with a smile as her fingers rattled across the keyboard.

'You'll get friction burn if you keep up that speed.' I was a bad person, but watching her frown and become irritable when I interrupted her was amusing me.

'Wha–? Oh, yeah, funny.' She smiled only with her mouth. 'I just want to get this down so I can send it to my agent, Natalie, once we get to Gran Canaria. She might give me notes straight away, and then I can keep working on it on the way to St Lucia.' Erin paused, as if waiting to see if I had anything else to say before she resumed her galloping pace.

I returned to my magazine, a smile playing on my face.

'How's the new book coming along?' Flick flopped down beside Erin and was trying to peer at the screen.

Erin huffed and snapped shut the laptop lid. 'It's fine. Sorry,' she said with a tight smile, 'I get a bit funny about people reading my work before it's finished.'

Flick responded with a tight smile of her own. 'Makes sense.'

I knew Erin hated talking to anyone about a working manuscript. Natalie was the only one allowed to discuss it with her. So I wasn't surprised when Erin changed the subject.

'Listen, I just wanted you to know, I completely understand why you flipped your lid about Bella being a part of the crew.'

'And how would you know anything about that?' Flick glared at Erin, any trace of friendliness vanished. I was as shocked as Flick. How the hell did Erin know anything about that? Jonty had very specifically told her he wasn't going to talk about it. Sean then? Or, Bella?

I heard the flush of the head and Flick turned to glare at Jonty as he emerged into the saloon.

'What?' He looked startled.

'Do you really have to tell everyone about your dirty little secret?'

It was as if everyone and everything froze in the cabin; we

braced for a vocal storm. Erin covered her mouth, trying to hide a smile. *What the hell was she playing at?*

'Flick, it–'

'Stay out of it, Erin.'

'I haven't told anyone anything. I told Erin it wasn't my story to tell,' Jonty said with a sigh. He looked at Erin, his eyes wide, as if encouraging her to back him up. 'Isn't that right?'

'Y-yes. It wasn't Jonty who told me.'

'Right, well it must have been that dirty little bitch then.' Flick stood up and began hammering on Erin and Bella's cabin door. 'Get out here, I want a word with you!'

Hugo, Sean and Nick had all opened their cabin doors and were now watching with interest and sharing shocked, but slightly amused looks.

The port cabin door opened slowly, and Bella filled the space, leaning against the frame. 'Can I help you?' Her serenity was to be applauded, but it only incensed Flick further.

'It's a bit late for that now, don't you think? Did you not get enough of a kick spreading your vile gossip around my friends, without having to do it here as well? I am stuck here, with you, for another three weeks and you couldn't just keep your big fat mouth shut, could you?'

I didn't dare move, I barely dared breath. Every muscle in Flick's body was tensed, her face beetroot and her hands in fists by her side. Part of me knew I should intervene, but I didn't.

Bella, more relaxed, but definitely angry, took a pace forwards; Flick didn't move. 'First of all,' Bella said in a low, abrupt voice, 'it wasn't gossip; it actually happened.'

'Pfft–'

'Second of all,' Bella raised her voice just enough to quiet Flick, 'the only person I ever said anything to, was you.'

'Bullshit!'

'It's true. Want to tell her the truth now, Jonty? Because if you don't, I will.' The razors in Bella's words could have cut the thickest of ropes.

All eyes turned towards Jonty, who was trying to back away, except there was nowhere to go. His face was pale and his Adam's apple bobbed up and down as he swallowed hard, trying to find the words. 'I…'

'What truth?' Flick was beginning to look as confused as I felt.

'Bella, you promised.' Jonty was pleading.

'I know I did, but I am not going to be spoken to like that and hated and ignored in this tiny space for the next however long until we get to St Lucia, especially when I have done absolutely nothing wrong.' Bella shouted the last three words and it took a few moments before anyone spoke again.

'Bella's right. She didn't do anything wrong. It was me.' Jonty could barely be heard above the sounds of the sea and wind coming from outside.

'Yes, we know that. Sort of. You were married, she wasn't. What's your point?' Flick threw her hands in the air.

'I told Bella that we'd separated. When she thought we were still together she didn't want anything to do with me.' Jonty's words came out in a rush. He swallowed hard and looked at the ceiling. 'The reason everyone found out was because I left my phone on the table. One of the guys was going to take some selfies as a laugh and found the pictures.'

I looked around, Bella was the only one smiling. But it wasn't a triumphant smile, it was a sad smile. She took no pleasure in outing Jonty, that much was clear. I understood her no longer being willing to be the bad guy and wondered why she'd held on so long. What did she owe Jonty?

'Perhaps the rest of this conversation should take place in private,' Nick suggested from his cabin doorway.

'Bit late for that now,' Flick said bitterly. She turned back to Jonty. 'You pretended we had split up so you could get laid? You lied, so you could get your leg over?'

I could see Flick's fury rise with each word she spoke. Jonty was now staring at the floor, his arms folded as if trying to make himself as small as possible. He nodded, mute.

'Of all the…' Flick spun to face Bella. 'Why didn't you just tell me it wasn't you?'

Bella shrugged. 'It didn't matter, not then anyway. It wasn't like we were friends and you needed to have some sort of relationship for the kids' sake. I didn't expect this,' she waved her arms around, 'to happen.'

Flick sat heavily as the boat was buffeted by a wave. 'I don't believe this,' she said, shaking her head.

'I'm a lot of things, but I don't do married men, just in case any of you were wondering.' Bella took a moment to look at each of us individually. 'If we're done here…?' She didn't wait for an answer before she turned back into her cabin and closed the door behind her.

'I–'

'Just fuck off, Jonty.'

Jonty pushed past Nick into the cabin they shared. Nick closed the door gently. 'I think I'll just give him a minute.'

Sean, Hugo and Nick came and joined Flick, Erin and me at the table.

'Well, that was…' Hugo said and everyone nodded in agreement.

'Flick, are you okay?' Nick asked.

'I'll be fine. I'm going to lie down.'

'Let me know if I can get you anything,' I said.

'I just want to be alone.'

The boys showed no signs of leaving the table. I had some questions of my own and now seemed as good a time as any since everyone seemed to be in truth-telling mode.

'Sean, did you know Bella before too?'

Sean and Hugo looked surprised, a little nervous even, while

Nick looked merely interested and switched his attention between us.

'I… How could you…' Sean paused. 'Sort of.'

I frowned and made a circular motion with my hand, encouraging him to continue.

'I met Bella on Plenty of Fish. Well, we chatted on Plenty of Fish, but we never actually met in real life. She wanted to meet up, she was a bit full on if I'm honest; kind of put me off a bit.' Sean dragged a hand over his shaved head. 'When my ex left me I was devastated, but mostly I was lonely. I chatted to a few women online, but they were all nutters, so I packed that in pretty sharpish. I couldn't believe it when she rocked up.'

I felt sorry for Sean. He was a nice guy and I could see some women might try to take advantage of that.

'Well, isn't this just the afternoon for sharing secrets,' Nick said jovially.

'Hmm.' I avoided eye contact. Some secrets were best left untold.

CHAPTER NINE

NOVEMBER – AFRICA AND THE CANARY ISLANDS

The remaining few days of the first leg of our trip passed without any further drama, which I was grateful for. After the Flick/Jonty/Bella outburst, I had a quiet word with Erin and asked her not to pry any further. She took offence to the word pry, but we both knew that's exactly what she was doing. That writer nose of hers had sniffed out some drama and she wanted to know the full story. She knew enough of it now, and I told her so.

The weather was fine, if a little on the windy side. But wind was good; it meant we arrived at the yacht club on the south coast of Gran Canaria in excellent time.

Gran Canaria sits right in the middle of the Canary Islands in terms of size and is home to Las Palmas, the party town of the island. Thankfully, we would be nowhere near it. Las Palmas was on the north shore at the opposite end of the island. I couldn't think of anything worse than having to navigate around twenty-something partygoers wearing next to nothing, who were smashed most of the time and didn't appreciate that some of us wanted a bit of peace and quiet. Judging by the excitement from some of the crew though, they had other ideas.

While Flick and Bella hadn't quite become best friends, the frosty atmosphere whenever they were in each other's vicinity had at least thawed. Jonty, however, was a different story. I would have expected Flick to direct her ire in his direction now, but instead she did the opposite; she pretended he didn't exist. And no amount of needling or cajoling on Jonty's part made the slightest bit of difference. Flick came to me and quietly explained that if there was any kind of emergency, she would obviously revert to being a team player, but until then, as far as she was concerned, Jonty hadn't made it on board. It didn't take him long to give up trying to talk to her.

We were due to spend four days in Gran Canaria, where it was a balmy twenty-four degrees. I wasn't a sun worshipper, but I really did despise cold, dull winter days and the nights even more. I often thought about moving somewhere closer to the equator: I could sail from anywhere after all, but I couldn't quite bring myself to leave Scotland permanently. I contented myself with sailing south during the winter months as often as I could.

Our four-day turnaround time was partly to get some proper rest before we embarked on the 3,400 nautical mile sail to St Lucia, but also to restock.

While we were tied up alongside in the little port, we needed to check our supply levels and calculate how much more food, water and fuel we would need for three weeks at sea. (Or even longer if the weather wasn't on our side.)

I also wanted the yacht to be cleaned from top to bottom, inside and out. Equipment, ropes and sails all needed to be checked as well. If anything went wrong while we were in the middle of the Atlantic, there was very little we could do and not a lot of help around. Our only methods of communication were the sat phone, and maybe the VHF radio, but that would only work if there were other vessels nearby. No matter *how* we were able to contact someone, it would still take days for anyone to get to us. The crossing was half as long as the diameter of the earth. I prayed to Neptune – my personal favourite god of the sea – that nothing went wrong.

While we were in port, mother watches continued as normal, but the whole atmosphere on board was much more relaxed since other crew members were free to help clean the boat and check the equipment.

After a long day sorting *Duchess* out, we were all sitting up top, lounging around with a drink and enjoying the sunshine. Flick and Hugo were down below preparing our evening meal; there was a beautifully chilled atmosphere and I was enjoying my first glass of wine in over a week.

'Do you know, I haven't really missed this,' Erin said quietly, nodding towards where her drink sat on the table in front of her.

'No?' I was pleasantly surprised. Erin had used alcohol as a crutch after Rhea died and I had been concerned enough to seek some advice from Alcoholics Anonymous. I could understand her need for oblivion, but I didn't want her to live there forever.

'No. I'm genuinely enjoying this, rather than drinking it as a means to an end.'

'That's really great to hear.' I squeezed her hand and smiled.

I leaned back on the sofa, eyes closed behind my sunglasses, and listened to the hum of the conversations going on around me. The sunshine warmed my face and I started to doze.

'Holy fuck! What are you doing?' Hugo's exclamation could be heard clearly on deck and was loud enough to jolt me from my snooze.

"It was an accident, help me put this out,' Flick snapped.

I was out of my seat quicker than Usain Bolt, but Nick was quicker.

'What's go–' I was cut off by a skooshing sound and saw Nick aiming the fire extinguisher at the stove top.

'What the hell is going on down there?'

I stepped back to allow Nick, Hugo and Flick back up the

stairs. Nick was trying not to laugh, and Hugo and Flick wouldn't look at anyone.

'What happened?' Jonty asked.

'What happened was, your ex-wife isn't any better at cooking now than when she was married to you.' Nick was laughing.

'Fuck off!'

Everyone else looked just as confused, I left it up to Hugo to explain. 'I went to the loo and left Flick in charge of dinner.'

There were groans all round.

'She set fire to our food,' Hugo finished.

'I did not set fire to it,' Flick said grumpily.

'So where exactly did the flames come from?' I was not messing around.

'It *caught* fire, there's a difference.' Flick had the same petulance we'd all come to associate with Carl.

'Well, whatever happened, the whole boat needs to be aired, and cleaned again. You better hope there's no damage either.' Paying for someone's idiocy was not on my agenda.

'It wasn't alight for that long,' Flick mumbled.

By now everyone was trying hard not to laugh, apart from me and Flick. However, I caught Nick's eye and somehow I cracked. I snorted and then so did someone behind me, and before I knew it we were all howling with laughter.

'No one was hurt, I suppose. But if there's any damage, I'm sure as hell not paying for it.' I couldn't stop giggling, but I was deadly serious.

'What are we going to do about dinner now Hugo and Flick have managed to destroy ours?' Sean asked.

'Hey!' Hugo punched his friend in the arm.

'Sorry dude, but she scares me way more than you.' Sean gestured towards Flick who rolled her eyes and poured herself some wine.

'Why don't I see if the tapas place can fit us in? It would be silly not to enjoy some of the local cuisine while we're here.' After a general murmuring of consent, Nick sat down next to me. 'Feed and water them, and they're always happy.'

———————

Nick had managed to secure a reservation for all ten of us after promising that we wouldn't rush the servers and we would relax and enjoy the evening.

I put on my smartest – cleanest – sailing clothes and reassured Erin she didn't need any kind of dress, day or otherwise. The place we were going to was more of a sailors' place anyway, and everyone would be dressed like yachties. The only locals would be the staff.

Despite the fact the staff at the restaurant had told us our order may take a while to prepare and cook, we were served quite quickly. Tapas was my kind of food. I could never make up my mind what I wanted to eat and having lots of small plates with all my favourites was perfect.

CHAPTER TEN

NOVEMBER – THE CANARY ISLANDS – DAY ONE

After we'd eaten and had a couple more drinks, we decided to move on to somewhere more lively. It wasn't my usual scene and I didn't often go out partying with my crew, but the others persuaded me it was what we all needed. Somewhere to let our hair down a bit before the gruelling, and no doubt tedious, Atlantic crossing.

'I'll go on one condition.'

'What's that?' Hugo was bouncing around in excitement.

'No one gets smashed. Yes, we can have a drink and have a good time, but we all have work to do tomorrow.'

'Fine, fine, we agree!' Hugo yelled, pulling me out of my seat by both hands. I laughed and allowed myself to be swept along by their giddy enthusiasm.

'What did Hugo say this place was called?' I asked Nick as we strolled along the path.

'It's called Isabella's. Hugo likes going there because there are usually lots of pretty young ladies for him to flirt with.' Nick rolled his eyes good-naturedly and I responded with a knowing smile. Hugo was definitely the Casanova of the group; the kind of sailor with a girl in every port.

The building housing the bar stood on its own, set back from the road, but there was no way you could miss it. The whole place was lit up like something on a tourist strip and I could hear the music from a hundred metres away. Suddenly I really didn't want to be here. Lively I could deal with, but this looked like my idea of hell.

'Um... I'm not sure...'

'It's not as bad as it looks, I promise,' said Bella over her shoulder.

'Still, I...' Suddenly the idea of an empty boat, the only sound the gentle lapping of the water, seemed appealing.

'Why don't you just come in and see what it's like? If you hate it, we can go back to the tapas bar and have a nightcap there.' Nick offered me his arm.

I looked towards the bar where Hugo stood, holding the door open and waving at us all to catch up. The others followed him in, arguing over whose round it was, while I tried to make up my mind.

'Come ON you two!' Flick ran back to where we stood and grabbed hold of our wrists, dragging us towards the door.

Decision made.

Inside there was a waist-level bar; I watched as two servers whirled around one another serving drinks to patrons with incredible efficiency. They moved as though they were involved in a complicated flamenco dance. But not once did they get in each other's way and neither were there any complaints about people not being served in order.

The source of the music was revealed in a far corner: a DJ complete with headphones was doing their thing on the decks. I was confused though, I couldn't see any records, just a laptop and lots of lights. I sighed, I was getting old.

Despite the bright lights intermittently illuminating the darkness, the crazy-loud music and the pirouetting bar staff, there was... space. I'd expected an overcrowded mass of heaving bodies fighting to get to where they wanted to be. Instead there were vacant booths and room for people to dance if they wanted to. Call me boring or old, but I hated having to balance my drink while I stood in a corner trying not to spill it at the same time as keeping out of everyone else's way.

The whole vibe of the place was chilled and welcoming. My shoulders floated down from my ears and my jaw unclenched.

'Okay?' Nick had to speak close to my ear so I could hear him.

I nodded, gave him my drink order and then made my way to where Bella, Erin and Flick had found us a seat.

'See? It's not so bad,' Bella shouted.

'It's better than I thought it would be, but still quite loud,' I yelled back.

Erin grimaced.

We cheered as the boys came back with our drinks. I took a long pull on my bottle of beer and settled into the cushioned chair-back. I had no desire to spend the rest of the evening shouting to be heard, and I was quite content to watch the others; Flick and Bella somehow managed to hold a conversation, and I wondered if they might become friends after all. Hugo and Sean had made their way to the dance-floor and looked as though they were trying to chat up a couple of local women, who were having none of it.

Carl though, was still standing by the bar, having tucked himself into a corner out the way. Like me, he appeared to be happy observing and didn't feel the need to join in. Or was it that he just didn't feel welcome? He was given a hard time by the others, but he also didn't do himself any favours.

Jonty sat on the end of the bench looking miserable. I wasn't sure why he'd decided to come with us if he was just going to sit around moping. Sure, Flick wasn't talking to him and he was unlikely to want to spend time with Bella, but he could dance with the boys, or chat to literally anyone else. Still, it was his problem if he wanted to exclude himself from the group and I didn't want him ruining my good mood, so I avoided eye contact and laughed at the dancing boys' efforts instead.

Between the wine at dinner and the two bottles of beer I'd drunk already, my bladder announced it was ready to be emptied. The ladies was across the other side of the bar and to get to it, I had to cross the dance-floor. I spent a few minutes eyeing the route suspiciously, wishing to hell there was a way around. It was no good, I just had to go for it.

I kept my head down and was grateful to my sensible deck shoes and whatever sticky liquid had been spilled, for making sure I didn't slide about all over the place.

On the way back I wasn't so lucky, Sean saw me coming, pointed at me and then cheered. I cringed; he thought I was coming to dance. He grabbed me by both hands, encouraging me to move. I tried, but I was convinced everyone was watching me and I hated being the centre of attention. The result was a kind of weird bobbing. *Christ!* Not wishing to be a party-pooper – there would be enough of that sort of thing when we were at sea – I broke free and pulled Erin up from the table; we could be silly together. She tried to pull back, but I wouldn't let go and yelled, 'Come on!' instead.

Back on the dance-floor Sean and Hugo surrounded us, dancing like lunatics and with a freedom I envied. I watched as Hugo grabbed hold of Erin's hands, pushing them back and forth, encouraging her to loosen up.

I glanced around, expecting a crowd of eyes to be staring and laughing at us. What I saw instead was people enjoying themselves, lost in their own good time, and not giving two shits what anyone else thought.

Fuck it, I thought, and joined in. When I was younger I loved a good cheesy disco and it felt like *so long* since I'd lost myself in the pleasure of music. Just for a little while, I wanted to forget all the shit and enjoy myself. I couldn't remember the last time I'd felt so relaxed.

'Get off me!' Erin was screaming at someone.

Hugo: he was dancing behind her, his armed wrapped round her waist and he couldn't see the fear on her face.

'Why've you stopped? Keep dancing!' he yelled back, oblivious to her panic.

Erin stepped forward to try and naturally break his hold, but he hadn't noticed. Grabbing hold of his wrists, Erin forced them apart and then threw them down. 'Get off me!' she screamed again. There was a millisecond break in the music just as she shouted and now people *were* staring.

'What? I was just mucking about. I thought you wanted to dance.' Hugo was still having to raise his voice, but he looked hurt.

'I-I'm sorry.'

'What's going on?' Suddenly Nick was there, looking concerned.

I stepped close to Erin and tried to pull her into a hug, but she shrugged me off.

'Are you okay?'

She looked like she was going to cry.

'Just a misunderstanding.' Hugo shrugged.

A misunderstanding? It had to be, Hugo was a good guy, but then I'd never seen Erin so freaked out.

'I need to go,' she said, and pushed her way towards the door.

I chased after her. By the time I got outside Erin had put some distance between herself and the bar. She was bent over, her hands on her knees, and breathing deeply.

'Hey. Are you okay?' I spoke from a few paces away, not wanting to give her a fright.

'I'm... I'm fine. Just got a little bit panicked, that's all.'

The lamplight glinted off the tears in the corners of her eyes.

'What happened?'

'Hugo came up behind me and put his arms round me. He wouldn't let go and I freaked out.'

'I'm sure he didn't mean anything by it.'

'That doesn't make it okay,' Erin snapped.

'Are you guys all right?' Flick handed us our bags. I'd forgotten all about them.

'Yeah. Just Hugo being a bit of a tosser.'

'Oh,' Flick's face twisted into understanding, 'yeah, he's a lot sometimes. Are you coming back in?'

'No, I'm going back,' Erin said.

'I'll come with you. How about that nightcap?' I smiled, trying to diffuse Erin's anxiety.

'Mind if I tag along? I'll just let the others know.'

'Sure.'

Erin folded her arms tightly around her stomach and scuffed her feet in the dirt while we waited for Flick to come back.

'Hugo says he's sorry, he never meant to upset you,' Flick said as we walked along the path back towards the marina.

'It's fine. Can we just forget about it?'

Back at the tapas bar the evening was still warm, so we opted to sit outside and enjoy the night air.

'So what exactly prompted you to embark on a trip across the Atlantic in a fifty-six-foot yacht?' Flick's question to Erin stirred me from my thoughts.

'It's kind of a long story and there's a couple of different parts to it.'

Flick checked her watch and then twisted her wrist. 'We have time.'

I watched Erin, checking to see if she was comfortable. Ready to step in if she looked like she might want to run again.

'The short version is, I just needed to get away. I needed some space to breath, to think, to escape what my life had become. I thought a change of... *everything* might kind of kick-start me again.' Erin looked solemn for a moment. 'Why did you want to come? Just to say you've done it?'

'That, and to prove I could. And to show I was more than just some yacht wife and mother.' Flick breathed the last words. 'Believe it or not, I married Jonty because I loved him. I was happy to be a wife and mother, and then he belittled everything I was by shagging Bella.'

Our dynamic was shifting. We'd entered a new level of friendship, acquaintanceship, call it what you like, but there were some deep feelings being shared.

'And *then* I was utterly humiliated by my so-called friends gossiping about it.'

'Have you forgiven Bella? I mean, we all know Jonty's still in the dog house.' I snorted.

'I know none of it was her fault now, but I hated her for so long, it's hard to let go completely. I just don't understand why she believed him so readily, you know? She didn't check or anything. Still, she wouldn't be the first person to believe whatever they wanted to believe.'

We were quiet for a while after that.

CHAPTER ELEVEN

GRAN CANARIA – DAY TWO

I rolled over and banged onto something hard. Snuffling and still half asleep, I rolled the other way, stretching an arm out. Underneath my fingertips I felt the warm skin of another person and snatched my hand back, suddenly very much awake.

I sat up, leaning on one arm and peered into the darkness, before flopping back down onto the bunk. Of course, I was at sea, on *Duchess*, in the Canary Islands. And this was why I wasn't really one for drinking. Erin, Flick and I had talked for hours and a quick nightcap on the way back to the yacht had become several.

My skin was clammy and my head fuzzy. I shouldn't have had that last drink. I snorted, yeah, it was definitely the last one that caused the problem, not all the others before that. It wasn't entirely my fault; Flick was the one who'd suggested another and I was enjoying myself too much to want to leave.

I stared up through the skylight above me, and groaned quietly. It was still pitch black outside; the sun wouldn't be up for a while yet.

I closed my eyes and tried to get comfortable, hoping to sleep through the hangover and come out the other side feeling fine. I tried to tune in to the sounds of ropes clanging from masts and the creaking as the boat eased in and out on the gentle swell. These were my comfort sounds and normally, once I focused on them, I would drop off easily, but just at that moment, Flick started snoring. I grabbed my pillow and pulled it down over my head, wishing I'd never had to share with her in the first place.

These were not cute, baby-lion-type snores either, these were full-on fat, alcoholic man snores, which given Flick's size and shape was astonishing.

There was no way I was going to get any more sleep now, so I decided to get up. I'd make a coffee and sit up on deck. It was rare to have solitary peace on board, and I welcomed the opportunity.

I checked the time while I waited for the kettle to boil. 6am, not as early as I'd thought. Sunrise wasn't all that far off.

The interior of *Duchess* wouldn't have been out of place in a five-star hotel it was so luxurious. I did pray for the white leather sofa though and double-checked to see if there were any marks from where Flick had burned the previous night's food. I nodded to myself, quietly impressed with what a great job they'd done of clearing up.

My coffee made, I grabbed some biscuits and opened the hatch to the deck as quietly as possible; bloody thing still squealed though and sounded even louder in the quiet space. Outside, the air was pleasant with little wind, and I settled myself and my thoughts in the cockpit, relishing the peace and quiet.

The sunshine and the prospect of a long sail ahead left me with a contented feeling. Things were finally going well.

Before long I heard movement from down below and I hunched down to see who else was awake. Erin soon appeared in the doorway to her cabin, rubbing sleep from her eyes, but otherwise looking refreshed. How, after the amount of wine she put away last night, I didn't know.

I made my way back down below.

'I didn't expect you to be up early this morning.'

'Insomnia doesn't seem to care how much I have to drink. Still,' she checked her watch, 'this is a lie-in for me.'

'Maybe try staying in bed? You're not going to be able to keep this up, and we can't have you falling asleep on watch.'

'I know. To be fair, I'm not sure the insomnia would let me anyway.' Erin changed the subject. 'More coffee?'

'Mm, please, that would be lovely.'

A few minutes later she placed a mug of steaming black coffee in front of me where I was sitting at the chart table. She sat on the sofa, her legs curled up underneath her.

We settled into a companionable silence and before long the sun slowly started to peek through the portholes and rouse the remaining crew. It felt gloriously warm on the side of my neck and I turned towards the porthole for maximum exposure.

The saloon and galley were soon a mass of people moving around to use the heads, brush their teeth, go for a shower and make themselves some breakfast.

'Hey, has anybody seen Hugo?' Sean poked his head out of the door to his cabin.

I twisted round in my seat to face him, glasses perched on the end of my nose. 'No, is he not in his bunk?'

'No.' Sean spoke slowly with extreme patience. 'If he were there then I wouldn't be asking, would I?'

'I've been up since about six, and I haven't seen him?'

'I don't think his bunk's been slept in,' Sean said.

Displaying a fit of pique, I threw my glasses on the chart table and rubbed the bridge of my nose. 'For fuck sake, I bloody told him not to get pissed!' I exploded and everyone in the saloon froze.

'Helen, I–' Nick started.

'Right, well, I suppose we'll need to waste some time finding him, won't we?' I said, cutting him off.

'I'll ring him, that seems like the easiest thing to do,' Sean said, soothingly.

'Fine, but tell him I want him back here pronto. There's work to be done. Speaking of which, I want everyone back in here for a briefing at 0830.'

There was no sign of Hugo at the briefing. I realised, belatedly, my hangover was making me grumpy, but I was too stubborn to care, or apologise.

Afterwards, I asked Erin to join me on deck and for the next few hours we went over what each of the ropes were called, what their purpose was, the names of the different sails, what different commands meant, what she should do in various situations; over and over again.

'Helen, we've been over this a million times.'

'Another couple won't do any harm.'

'But I might do some harm to you,' she mumbled – except she was loud enough to make sure I heard her. 'I know you're annoyed about Hugo, but I don't think it's fair you make me your distraction.' Erin's words penetrated my stubbornness.

'I'm sorry, you're absolutely right. I do wish we'd managed some more training trips before we left Scotland though.'

'I *know* you do; you've told me enough times. But we were both busy and there's nothing can be done about it now.' Erin's patience was worn out.

Although it was November, we were significantly closer to the equator in Gran Canaria, which meant I was getting quite sweaty working on deck. I checked my watch, it had to be nearly–

'Lunchtime!'

'Right, let's get this equipment put away and then we can eat,' I said. 'Jonty's making lunch today, so at least we know it'll be edible.' I rolled my eyes in an exaggerated fashion, hoping Erin might forgive me and laugh along. 'And maybe Hugo will turn up. If it's not his dick running his life, then it's his stomach.'

CHAPTER TWELVE

GRAN CANARIA – DAY TWO

That afternoon we had some free time and rather than sit on *Duchess*, stewing about where Hugo was, I decided to go for a walk. Although the marina wasn't particularly close to any actual towns, it was like a little village in itself. I headed to the bar where we had eaten last night; there was plenty of outdoor seating from where I could watch the world go by.

I settled myself at a table near the door and pulled out my phone to check the weather for the next few days, even though I knew exactly what it was going to say. As expected, the winds were good and there was no sign of rain.

'Hola, señora, a drink?'

I briefly considered ordering a glass of wine, but given the state of me the previous night, my foul mood this morning *and* the fact I was missing a crew member, I decided against it. *'Café con leche, por favor.'*

The server's smile was somewhere between pleased I'd tried to speak Spanish and amused at my awful accent. He left to complete my order and from behind the safety of my sunglasses I observed my fellow patrons.

The problem was, when you'd listened to one yachty word-vomit endlessly about the Round the Island Race, you'd listened to them all. I really needed to go on a proper holiday, away from sailor types and somewhere I could actually relax. Meet new people and talk about something other than weather fronts, currents and tides.

My mind wandered to Hugo and where he was.

I texted Sean to ask if Hugo had turned up yet. His reply was swift.

> No – I'm getting a bit worried. I know he likes to put it about a bit, but he's normally up and out the door well before his latest conquest wakes up in case she suggests breakfast or something.

I replied saying there was probably nothing to worry about, but perhaps we ought to have a scout round the bars to see if we could see him anywhere. In reality, I *was* worried.

> Do you think he might've started drinking again? Wouldn't put it past him. Where are you? We can look for him together. I've got a pic on my phone we can show people. I'm gonna kill him when I find him.

I told Sean where I was and settled my bill while I waited for him.

A couple of hours later, Sean and I had searched everywhere we could think of and lost count of the number of people we had shown Hugo's photograph to. There were a few who seemed to know Hugo; he was a prolific sailor and came to Gran Canaria often, but no one could say with any certainty they had seen him the evening before. Even the bar where we'd been drinking with the others after dinner hadn't yielded any results.

'Might he have decided to get a cab to the town further up the coast?' I said, spotting one idling across the road.

'I mean, it's possible, but why isn't he answering his phone?'

'It could've run out of charge?'

'True, but why is he still not back? Even if he didn't have any money, the Hugo I know would turn up in a cab and persuade someone else to pay for it. This just isn't like him.'

'Shall we go back to the yacht? Catch up with the others? You never know, he might be back by now.'

His face grim, Sean agreed.

'Did you find him?' Bella was sitting in the cockpit with a cuppa.

'No. I'm worried now. Even for Hugo this is odd.'

'I agree. I think it's time to call the police, don't you?'

'Yeah.'

I took control of the situation. I don't think anyone even considered that they should volunteer; I was *Duchess*'s skipper after all.

'The police said they'll be here within the hour. I'll go and meet them up at the marina office in a bit. I expect they'll want to speak to everyone.'

The previous day's joviality had disappeared and we spread out around the boat. Misery might love company, but apparently us humans didn't.

'Do you want me to come with you?' Sean asked.

'No, I'm good, thanks.'

I climbed down from *Duchess* and walked slowly along the pontoon, my eyes on the wooden planks before me. *Where was he?* There was a part of me that feared the worst. I pushed the thought away and made my way up to the marina office.

I didn't have to wait long for the police to arrive. Reports of a missing foreigner, even if they weren't technically a tourist, were not good for the island's reputation. It was in the police's best interests to act quickly.

'*Hola, buenas tardes.* Señora Johnstone?'

'Hola, yes, that's me.'

'It was you who reported a missing member of your crew?' The policeman switched seamlessly to English.

'Yes, it was. Hugo. We don't think he came back to the boat last night.'

'I see. My name is Sub-inspector Alcaraz and this is Polícia Ramos.' He placed one hand on his chest and bowed very slightly.

'Nice to meet you.' It wasn't, but I could be painfully British in stressful situations. 'Shall we go back to *Duchess* and then you can talk to everyone together?'

'*Si.* Please.' Sub-inspector Alcaraz held a hand out in front of him, gesturing for me to lead the way.

Back on board I asked everyone to gather down below and the crew crammed themselves onto the sofa. I took up my usual position behind the chart table. It made me feel like I was in control – something of a crutch. The two police officers stood in the galley, their notebooks out.

'Who would like to tell us what happened?' Sub-inspector Alcaraz asked in his accented English.

Everyone looked at me, clearly expecting me to answer first. I took the hint. 'Sean, why don't you explain. You're his best mate and you were with him last night.'

'Sure, the last time I saw Hugo was in Isabella's last night. He wasn't ready to leave when I was, so I left him to it. Everyone else had already gone.' Sean shrugged. 'He knows this place like the back of his hand, I didn't think anything of it.'

'What time did you leave?' Sub-inspector Alcaraz asked.

'I couldn't say for certain, but it must have been round midnight I suppose.'

'Please, continue.'

And he did, but there wasn't much left to tell. Sean explained about trying to call Hugo and our search this afternoon. The rest of us filled in pieces of information we thought might be relevant, but beyond giving the police a photograph and Hugo's telephone number, there wasn't much to say.

'You should tell them what happened with you and Hugo,' Flick said during a lull.

'I really don't think it's relevant.' Erin looked horrified.

'What happened?' After a few moments of silence, the policeman tried again. 'Please, señora, we should decide what is or isn't relevant.'

'Honestly, it was just a misunderstanding and I over-reacted.' Both the police officers remained silent, watching Erin patiently. 'Fine!' Erin explained what had happened, playing it down as much as she could, while Polícia Ramos scribbled in his notebook.

Afterwards, the officers asked us all a few questions separately. How did we know Hugo? Did we know anyone who might hold a grudge? That sort of thing. They also spent far too long on the dance-floor incident. But by the time they had finished questioning me, I felt utterly useless. I liked the guy, but I realised I barely knew him.

Our evening meal was eaten in silence, not that anyone had much of an appetite.

'Does anyone else want a glass of wine?' Erin stood and shuffled into the galley.

'Do you not think alcohol has caused enough problems already?' I snapped.

Erin froze, eyes like Bambi.

'It's just a glass of wine, Helen,' Nick said softly.

'But it's never just one glass, is it?'

'It doesn't matter.' Erin put the bottle back in the fridge, her face red.

'I'm going for a walk.' I snatched up my mobile and sunglasses, and left in a hurry.

I stormed along the pontoon in anger. No idea where I was going, but I knew I needed to get away and just... walk. I pounded the pavement for over half an hour before the ire dissipated enough for me to walk at a normal speed. After that I wandered with my thoughts. I should never have let them go to that bar; I should never have gone with them. I should've been sober sister and checked everyone got back on board safely.

It was much later when I returned to *Duchess*. I climbed down the stairs and stood in front of the saloon table. 'I'm sorry, Erin. I was out of order before.'

She looked taken aback, glancing at the others. I could understand her surprise, I rarely apologised; I was rarely wrong, usually so measured and considered.

My phone rang. I answered and listened, only speaking when necessary.

'What's wrong?' Nick stood up.

'That was the police. They've found a body.'

CHAPTER THIRTEEN

'A body? What? They don't think it's Hugo, do they?'
I stared at the phone, not hearing Erin's questions properly. Guilt washed over me as I remembered how grumpy I'd been about Hugo earlier that morning. Why did I always think the worst of people? Yes, he could be a bit of a liability on a run ashore, but he took his responsibilities on board seriously, even if that wasn't always obvious to people who didn't know him well. And now... this.

'Helen! For God's sake, what did the police say?' Erin made sure I heard her this time.

'They, um... Hang on, let's get everyone in here. I don't want to have to say this twice.' I knew saying it once was going to be hard enough, I did not want to have to repeat myself. I raised my voice. 'Can everyone come to the saloon, please?' I listened for movement from the cabins and then climbed a few steps and stuck my head through the hatch. 'Can you all come down here for a minute?'

I stood in the galley, not making eye contact and silently practising what I was going to say.

'What's going on?' Carl asked.

'The police called Helen.' Erin spoke for me.

I turned to face them and quickly began speaking before she could say any more. I had the full attention of eight faces, each etched with varying degrees of worry.

'They did. They believe they've found Hugo–'

'Is he okay?' Sean was Hugo's best friend and I could see he was willing me to say yes, but fearing the worst.

'No, he's not. He's really badly injured.'

'You said they'd found a body!' Erin shrieked.

'I know, sorry, not the right word. They've found a man, unconscious, on the other side of the marina. He's been taken to hospital and they're pretty sure it's Hugo. They've asked me to go to the hospital, to confirm it for them.'

A tsunami of questions followed.

'What happened?'

'Will he be okay?'

'Is he awake?'

'Will we still be taking the yacht?'

I held up my hands, appealing for calm. 'I know as much as you do, other than, he's not awake yet.'

'When are you going to the hospital?' Sean asked.

'The police are sending a car for me now.'

'I'm coming with you.'

I opened my mouth to tell him it didn't need two of us, but he cut me off. 'That wasn't a question, Helen. Yes, you are captain, but he's my best mate and I'm going.'

I stared at him for a few seconds and realised there was nothing to be gained by arguing. 'Fine, get ready. We'll head up to the office and meet them.'

I stared out of the window as we drove along the coast of the island, the North Atlantic stretching out before me. Watching the constant, rhythmic, rolling ocean swell had helped to calm the emotions roiling inside me, as it often did. What if Hugo died before we got there? Would I be expected to identify a body instead of a John Doe?

Sean and I spoke very little in the back of the police car. What was there to say? Hugo's condition was too serious for us to even bother trying to offer up false comfort.

On arrival at the hospital, we were taken to the intensive care ward and shown to a bed at the end of a row. The room was simultaneously a cacophony of beeps and whooshing noises, and a strange, eerie silence. Our small party of four; me, Sean, Polícia Ramos and the nurse, were the only conscious people in the room.

As we approached the bed, and the patient's head and face came into view, despite the bandages and the tubes and the wires, I could clearly see it was Hugo. Paler than I remembered him, but definitely Hugo. I turned to Sean to see if he had recognised him too; his stricken face and watery eyes confirmed he had.

Sean approached the bed and, sitting on a nearby chair, reached for Hugo's hand. This tender moment between two best friends brought tears to my own eyes.

The policeman who had escorted us coughed discreetly, attracting my attention. I turned, his eyes asking a silent question. I nodded in answer, not wanting to break the church-like reverence around me.

The policeman tilted his head towards the door, and I followed him to the nurses' station. Giving Sean some privacy, I wanted him to have as long as possible with his friend.

'The doctors have said he was still unconscious when he arrived and there is some serious swelling on his brain. They have put him in a medically induced coma until the swelling goes down.'

'Is he going to be okay?'

'They will need to do some more tests once the swelling is reduced, until then, they cannot say.'

I nodded, lost with my thoughts for a moment. 'Do you have any idea what happened?'

'We don't know for sure, but he was found at the bottom of some concrete steps. We don't know if he fell, or he was pushed.'

'He was drunk, so isn't it likely that he fell?'

'Yes, but there are also what look like, defensive wounds on his hands. But they *could* also be as a result of the fall.'

'Oh my god.'

'We're checking CCTV and asking all the people who were on board their boats if they saw or heard anything, but there aren't that many moorings over there.'

'What was he doing over there anyway? *Duchess* is on the other side of the marina.'

'We're trying to find the answer to that too.'

Knowing the crew would have a hundred questions once we returned, I asked to speak to the doctor in charge of Hugo's case. I wanted to have as much knowledge as possible before we left. I'd always been the same, being aware of all of the information has always helped me deal with any given situation.

As we descended the steps below deck, Sean and I were faced with seven worried and impatient people.

'Is it him?' Jonty spoke first.

Sean nodded. 'Yeah, it's him.'

There were gasps and *oh shit*s from everyone.

'What have the police said?' Erin asked.

'Can someone get the wine out? I need a drink.'

Nick did the honours and I was grateful no one mentioned my outburst from before. Sean and I filled everyone in on what the police had said.

'So they think someone attacked him? That's mental.' Carl shook his head.

'They don't know anything for certain, but they think so. They're still making enquiries,' I replied.

'What was he doing round there anyway?' Flick was on the same wavelength as me.

'I wondered the same thing, but the police have no answers at the moment. They did say we may need to wait for Hugo to wake up.'

'He will wake up then?' Erin might have only known Hugo a short time, but she was just as concerned as the rest of us.

'That's something else they can't say for certain, but they'll know more once the swelling's gone down a bit.'

'How long will that take?' Connor asked.

'I spoke to the doctor before we left the hospital and here's what I know. Hugo has a bleed on his brain, which is causing pressure inside his skull. They have him on a load of different drugs, some to keep him in a coma and some to help with his injury. They need to release the pressure in his head and once the swelling has gone down they'll try to bring him out of his coma.

'Apparently you can only keep a person in an induced coma for a few days, no more than a week. If they need longer then it usually means their injuries are so severe they might never recover, or if they do, they are going to need significant care for the rest of their life.

'The doctors won't know anything for a few days. We just have to wait.'

There were a few moments of silence while everyone absorbed what I'd told them, and ordered it in their own minds.

'If Hugo wakes–'

'When! When Hugo wakes up,' Sean interrupted Bella.

'Sorry, you're right, Sean. *When* Hugo wakes up, is he likely to remember what happened?'

'The doctor I spoke to said with these types of brain injuries, anything could happen. Hugo will likely need to relearn a few things, but only time will tell if his memories return fully. Most likely, because of the way memories are stored in the brain, his long-term memory will come back first and then perhaps – hopefully – his short-term memory will also return.'

I waited to see if there were any more questions. I hoped not. I was mentally and physically exhausted; I didn't want to do any more talking right now.

'So what happens with the delivery?'

'Carl! How can you even think about that right now?' Flick glared at him.

'This probably isn't the time to be discussing it, but Carl's right, it's something I need to think about. Figure out.' No one mentioned my uncharacteristic defence of Carl. He'd saved me from having to bring up the subject myself.

Before I could elaborate a voice called from outside.

'Hello! Hello! Is anyone there, *Duchess?*'

CHAPTER FOURTEEN

Sean beat me to the stairs, haring up them in front of me. I could sense, rather than hear, the curiosity of the others behind me. I wasn't surprised when Carl appeared by my side: he always was a nosey git and never too proud to hide it either.

From the cockpit, I could see a young Spanish-looking woman with a bruise across her left cheek and eye, standing on the jetty; Sean seemed to know her.

'What's going on?' I asked.

'I'm looking for Hugo,' the woman said.

'And you are?' I tensed, immediately on guard. This was far too much of a coincidence for my liking.

'This is Liliana, she works at Isabella's. The bar where we all went after dinner last night.' Sean added the last bit on seeing the confusion etched across my face.

'I heard someone was asking for him. Where is he?' Liliana's accent was obvious, but her English excellent. A result of spending a lot of time serving tourists and sailors no doubt.

There was something else in her eyes I couldn't quite place. Was Hugo responsible for the purple-and-blue bruise across one side of her face? I dismissed the thought immediately; Hugo was a lover, not a fighter.

Whatever the truth of the matter, she deserved our compassion.

I waited for Sean to say something, but words seemed to fail him.

'Why don't you come on board?' I suggested.

Liliana looked back and forth between us, like perhaps she was waiting for Sean to add something. When finally he nodded, she climbed aboard and we took seats in the cockpit. I sent Carl back down below, Liliana didn't need an audience. I closed the hatch away from prying ears; as much good as that would do.

'Please tell me what's going on.' She addressed Sean directly and he took her hand in both of his. I found it an oddly intimate gesture – he knew Liliana well.

'Hugo's in the hospital, Liliana. I'm sorry.'

Liliana gasped: her English may be near-perfect, but her mannerisms were all Spanish. 'But how? What happened?'

Sean turned a little to look at me, his eyes pleading. I had no idea what was going on, or who this woman was to Hugo, but Sean's unspoken request for help was clear. If he needed me to do the explaining, then I would.

'Hugo had an accident last night,' I explained as gently as I could. 'He has a traumatic brain injury and the doctors have had to put him in a coma.' I realised, belatedly, there were a couple of words in there she may not have come across in her capacity serving beer to sailors. 'Do you understand what I'm saying?'

Liliana nodded slowly. 'It's all my fault,' she whispered.

I looked sharply at Sean who shrugged a little and shook his head. I nodded back at him, urging him silently to find out more.

'How could it possibly be your fault? He either fell, or someone attacked him and I know you didn't attack him.' Without waiting for her to reply, Sean turned to me and spoke again. 'Liliana and Hugo have been… seeing each other, on and off, for years now.'

Ah! Things were starting to make sense, but it still didn't explain why Liliana thought Hugo's accident was her fault. I waited for her to explain what she meant, but she started to cry. I pulled some tissues out of my pocket, handed them over and waited for her to calm down.

After a few minutes, once the tears had stopped and Liliana had composed herself, Sean tried again. 'What makes you think Hugo's accident was anything to do with you?'

Liliana closed her eyes, took a deep, fortifying breath and said, 'I think Mateo might have hurt him.'

'Who's Mateo?' I asked. I rarely went anywhere with the crew, preferring the quiet of the yachts I sailed over loud bars, but it meant I didn't really know who anyone was.

This time Liliana looked directly at me. 'Mateo is the man who wants to marry me. I have told him no many times, but he insists I am his. Somehow he found out I had been with Hugo last night and he lost his temper. He hit me and then stormed out of my flat vowing he was going to find Hugo and kill him.' She started crying all over again and Sean pulled her into a hug.

Momentarily stunned, I found I couldn't formulate a response. This… Mateo, seemed to think Liliana was somehow his property? Did people really still think in those terms? Liliana's theory made perfect sense though.

There was nothing else for it. I pulled out my phone and called the police. 'Hello? Yes, this is Helen Johnstone, the captain of the *Duchess*. There is a young lady here by the name of Liliana who may have some information regarding Hugo Marshall's accident.'

The police confirmed they would send someone round to ask some questions and take a statement. After I ended the call, I turned back to Liliana and Sean to explain what the police had said. Liliana was glaring at me.

'You should not have called the police.' She spat the words.

'Why not? You have information that might help find who did this to Hugo, if it wasn't an accident.'

'Mateo will be angry; look what he already did to me.'

'That's even more of a reason to get the police involved.'

'It's okay Liliana, we'll look after you. He won't be able to get anywhere near you while you're here.' Sean's tone was gentle. He was so much better at this stuff than I was and it made me care for him just that little bit more.

'And what happens when you go? I will still be here and he will still be here.' Whether Liliana was choked with fear, anger or both I couldn't be sure. Had I done the right thing?

'Let's just see what happens when the police arrive.'

'I'll get someone to rustle us up a hot drink.' I wasn't helping, so I decided to give them some space and do something practical. Physical help was more my forte. As I planted my feet on solid floor down below, I became aware all eyes were on me.

'What's going on?' Erin asked.

I considered how much to tell them for a moment; whether to tell them anything at all. Realising it didn't matter, I briefly explained about Liliana while I made the drinks.

'But Hugo was flirting with just about any woman who moved last night!' Erin exclaimed.

'I don't think that's really the point here, Erin,' Jonty said disdainfully.

'Well, no, but–'

'And I definitely don't think it's something Liliana needs to hear either. By the sounds of it, she has enough going on,' Jonty interrupted.

I fobbed off any further questions and promised to discuss it later once Liliana had gone and there was no chance she might overhear.

Back up on deck, I found Sean pleading with Liliana not to leave.

'The police are going to come and talk to you regardless. It's not as if they don't know where to find you.' Sean sounded exasperated.

'Liliana, please stay and tell the police what you know.' I set our drinks on the table. 'Whatever has happened, I'm fairly certain Hugo didn't deserve this.'

'And what if it was an accident and nothing to do with Mateo?'

'Even if that is the case, Mateo's not going to hurt you now, not when the police are involved.'

Liliana snorted.

I groped around in my mind, frantically trying to come up with more arguments for her to stay. Thankfully, the police arrived more quickly than I had anticipated. Liliana saw them coming and slumped in the seat, her head in one hand, defeated.

The police left about an hour later after taking Liliana's statement and photographing her injuries. This was all done in Spanish, which made sense, but I was frustrated. I had no idea if she'd given them any extra information in addition to what she'd told us.

They asked Sean and me about Mateo, and while I had no idea who he was, Sean admitted he did know of him.

'Why did you not tell us about him before?'

'I've never seen a bad side to him. It didn't even cross my mind he might be involved. He must be pretty good at hiding his temper. And Liliana always seemed to have the situation under control.' Sean glanced at Liliana, who nodded.

The police officer nodded once in response before closing his notebook and climbing down onto the jetty. He promised to be in touch once they had found and spoken with Mateo.

'I'm going to take Liliana home. I won't be long,' Sean said.

I sat in the cockpit and watched them walk up the jetty; Sean with an arm around Liliana and her head on his shoulder.

I spent a few moments gathering my thoughts and trying to make a plan for what we needed to do next. Not delivering on my contract to sail *Duchess* to St Lucia was not an option. I needed the payday and I couldn't even consider what might happen if I didn't get the money I was expecting.

In all reality, if I didn't want to lose money or fall too far behind – and frankly neither of these things was an option – there was only one thing I *could* do. I pulled out my phone, found the contact I was looking for and with a deep breath, I pressed the call button.

'I need you to come to Gran Canaria and help me sail a yacht to St Lucia.'

'I wondered if you'd call.'

'Well, I am calling. Are you coming?'

'I'll book a flight.'

CHAPTER FIFTEEN

There was no way I could afford to lose any of the five grand I was being paid to make sure *Duchess* arrived in St Lucia safely and on time. The vast majority of it was going to pay off debts and I couldn't afford to fall behind on my repayments.

I wasn't looking forward to breaking the news to the crew. They all knew Danny and none of them would be happy. My other son, Connor's twin – thankfully not identical – was not the kind of person most people wanted around. But he was an experienced sailor and although I hated to admit it, I needed him. Whatever kind of man he was, I was his mum and helping me was hardwired into him. In the same way it was in a mother's DNA to love and support her children – even if they sometimes did bad things.

It was well known that I didn't like to have to say the same thing twice, so I decided to wait until Sean arrived back on board and gave myself some breathing space.

The noise of the hatch being drawn back caught my attention. It was Erin.

'You okay up here?'

'Yeah, just doing some thinking.'

'Where's Sean?' Erin looked around. 'I thought he'd be here with you.'

'He's taken Liliana home. He won't be long.' I tried to hug myself and was surprised to find I wished it was Sean's arms wrapped around me.

'Dinner's nearly ready. We wondered if we could eat up here? It's a lovely evening and, well... we've all been down below for a while now.'

A shard of guilt sliced through me. Part of being here was to allow the crew a bit of freedom and the chance to move around before the long stretch across the Atlantic. 'Of course. Yes, absolutely. That's a great idea.'

Everyone busied themselves trying to be helpful. Passing plates and cutlery up the stairs, pouring drinks for one another. It made me a little sad that it had taken the near death of a crewmate to bring them together like this. It also made me question my abilities as skipper. Yes, I could get this boat from any A to B you wanted, but my people skills had always left something to be desired. And they were about to be tested to the limit. I hoped when I told them who was flying in to take Hugo's place their camaraderie would see us through. I suspected it was a forlorn hope though.

Sean returned and we all enjoyed a quiet meal of chicken-and-chorizo paella cooked by Nick, assisted by Erin. Technically it wasn't their turn, and technically it wasn't a traditional paella, but it was Nick's speciality and he said it had helped to take his mind off things. Perfect comfort food.

After we'd eaten Flick and Bella cleared the plates and washed up together. I knew once they'd finished I couldn't delay any longer. The paella suddenly lay heavy in my stomach; it was time to confess.

'I don't mean to sound insensitive, but what are we going to do about replacing Hugo?' Jonty spoke before I could find the words and there were murmurs of agreement all round.

'I have a plan, let's wait for the girls to finish and then I can tell you all together.' My answer seemed to satisfy them, but Connor gave me a funny look and I wondered if he guessed.

Fifteen minutes later we were all still sitting around the cockpit table, our drinks refreshed and it was time.

'Right, so,' I said, raising my voice a little to interrupt them. 'Obviously with Hugo in the hospital we need to find someone else to help us crew. Bearing in mind that we can't really afford any major delays, I have made a decision.' All eyes were on me, no one spoke. 'I have asked Danny–' I was immediately cut off by a chorus of loud groans and shouts of, 'No!'

'Are you serious?' I could normally rely on Nick to have my back, but even he couldn't believe what I'd done.

'I know what you all think of him and, I might be his mum, but I'm not an idiot, even I know he can be a… pain.'

'A pain? Calling Danny a pain is like saying drinking bleach might make you feel sick. I can't believe you'd have him on your crew, especially without asking us. You're fucking out of order, Helen!'

I leaned back away from Erin's explosion. Shocked by it. No, Danny would not necessarily have been my first choice, had I had a choice, but Erin's vehemence was out of proportion.

I wasn't kidding anyone: I knew and they knew, Danny was bad news.

'Look, I know how you all must be feeling. I had no other options.'

'Even if she did overreact a little, Erin's right. Don't you think it's something you should have discussed with us first?' Jonty was trying to be calm and pragmatic, but all he did was fire up my temper.

'What difference would it have made? How many people do you know who are capable of sailing across the Atlantic, who can drop everything at a moment's notice and be on an aeroplane within a couple of hours? Anyone who's experienced enough to fill Hugo's shoes, and wants to do it, is already crewing. Every single one of you knows that.' I made a point of looking at each of them individually. 'Taking the time to discuss it would have only meant more delays we can't afford, but the same outcome. All I've done is save us a few hours.'

'Where's he sleeping?' Sean glared at me, daring me to tell him they would be bunking together in Hugo's absence. I opened my mouth to speak, but he cut me off. 'And do *not* tell me he'll be sharing with me. I'd rather share with Carl.'

'Hey!' Carl was indignant. Sean shrugged.

'Well, that answers that then, doesn't it? Sean and Carl will share the aft cabin, Danny and Connor will share the bunks.' I dared not look at Connor. I knew he'd be furious, but because he was my son, I also knew he wouldn't say anything. At least not while the others were around. Connor and Danny were not the close, knew-what-each-other-was-feeling, kind of twins. As fraternal rather than identical twins, they didn't even look alike.

People expected twins, even fraternal twins, to be best friends, to have some kind of special link. Nothing could be further from the truth when it came to my two. They were different in every way possible: looks, hair, hobbies, personality and just about anything else you could think of.

Where Connor was kind, quiet and introverted, Danny was loud, brash and aggressive. Connor was fair and Danny was dark. Connor liked to read and spend time by himself, whereas Danny thought reading was for girls and was at his happiest surrounded by sycophants – I refused to call them friends – in the pub where they gave him their undivided attention. Connor was loyal, and Danny was only out for himself – yet demanded loyalty from those around him. It was Connor's loyalty that kept him quiet when I announced he would be sharing with his brother.

'When's he arriving?' Sean asked matter-of-factly.

'He's sorting out the logistics as we speak, but it looks like he'll be here by tomorrow evening. He'll let me know once he's booked his flight.'

'Well, we might as well enjoy the next twenty-four hours then. Who wants another drink?'

'Not for me, I'm going for a walk.' I needed to put some distance between myself and their vitriol. Their apparent hatred of Danny was tough for a mother to bear. I didn't want to listen to their rhetoric, nor pretend to not see their side-eye looks in my direction. He was still my son after all.

'Me neither,' Connor replied and for a moment I thought he might say he was going to join me. 'I'm going to read.' He stared at me, sending me a message. What it was exactly, I couldn't tell you – hurt, bitterness, anger, resentment, all of them? Whatever it was, he didn't want me anywhere near him, that much was obvious. It was fine by me, I didn't want to be around anyone right now anyway.

Erin was sitting on the edge of the bench, her arms folded tightly across her chest. Were they tears?

'Are you okay, Erin?' It was a tentative question, but I couldn't leave without checking. Tears had been a part of Erin's life for a long time now, but I hated the thought that I'd caused her pain somehow.

She glared up at me and I waited for her to speak. I couldn't understand the sheer anger emanating from her. Pissed off I could understand, but this was something else.

'I need to be alone,' she said through clenched teeth and then stormed past me and up onto the deck.

CHAPTER SIXTEEN

SETTING SAIL FROM GRAN CANARIA

We were due to leave Gran Canaria that evening. I had made the desperately difficult call to Hugo's parents informing them he had been attacked. I ended the call as quickly as politeness allowed, leaving them with Sub-inspector Alcaraz's contact information if they had more questions. Leaving Hugo behind felt strange, yet there was nothing to be gained by us staying.

Danny had been a member of our crew for a little over twelve hours and already I felt as if the end of our voyage could not come quickly enough. The atmosphere on board had become toxic, and even those who usually got along were snapping at each other. It was going to be a long three weeks. Despite my questionable people skills, I had to at least try and do something about it. I called a crew meeting.

'First things first: the weather and the tides all look good, so we will be setting sail this evening as planned. A bit of swapping around of watches – Nick, you'll now be with Flick. Jonty, you and Danny will be together.' I waited, daring someone to question me. My glare seemed to work and no one made any comment.

There was no way I could make Flick work with Danny. She recoiled if he came within a foot of her, which happened often on a sailing yacht, even one as big as this. I knew Jonty could handle him, though.

I took a deep breath. 'I realise that if we had the choice there would be some people here we would not choose to crew with. I get that, this wasn't how it was planned. However, this is how it's played out and now we have to get on with it. You all – *we* all – need to make an effort to get along and put our differences aside, otherwise this is going to be a really long, boring and stressful journey for everyone.' I paused to allow my words to sink in. 'Hopefully, between watches, sleeping, downtime, and mother watch, we'll all have enough space. Don't forget, the weather is going to keep getting better, so you can make use of the cockpit, or even the foredeck if needs be.'

Danny was grinning, amused by the fact he was the main reason for my words. He knew no one liked him and he couldn't have cared less. If I didn't think it would make things worse, I would have called him on it then and there. I scowled at him; he rolled his eyes. Everyone else was looking at the floor, or out of the nearest porthole. They were here, they were listening, but they weren't going to make it easy.

I sighed, defeated. 'The morning is yours. If you're not going to be here for lunch please let mother watch know. I need you all back on board by 3pm for final checks and ready to sail at 5.30. If you're on an overnight watch, please try to get some sleep.' I waited for some sort of confirmation I had been heard – nothing. Picking my battles was going to be the only way to help get me through the next three weeks. 'Fine, you can go.'

I swivelled my knees under the chart table so people could get past without banging into my legs. I put my glasses on and pretended to analyse the charts again. I didn't need to, I knew the route like the back of my hand, but I didn't want to catch anyone's evil eye as they left.

'Are you okay?'

I looked up. Sean and Nick were standing beside me, concern on their faces.

'I'm fine. This stuff goes with the skipper's hat.' I tried a reassuring smile.

'We know that,' Nick said quietly, 'but this is a lot for anyone.'

I stared at them, wondering when it would sink in that their reaction, their behaviour, was also adding to my load.

'For what it's worth, I'm sorry. I know we should be more supportive, but, well, you know...' Sean's half an apology was well-meaning.

'Me too.' Nick and Sean exchanged a look. 'We'll try harder and we'll have a chat with the others, but no promises. If Danny behaves like a prick, we're not pulling any punches.'

'Thank you. I'll have a word with Danny. I'm not sure how much help it'll be, but I can at least try.'

Sean gave my arm a squeeze and smiled. 'What are you doing now?'

'I'm going to finish up here and go for a walk.'

'Do you want some company?' Sean asked.

'Sure.'

'I'm going to go and see if Erin wants to get some lunch. She said there was a little bistro she wanted to try before we left.' Nick flushed.

I smiled fondly. 'Would you...' How could I put it? 'Could you make sure she's okay for me? Her reaction yesterday, it was... a lot. And definitely out of character.' Erin's tongue-lashing was still fresh in my mind and as much as I wanted to talk to her about it, she'd been avoiding me.

'Of course,' Nick said, squeezing me gently by the shoulder, before climbing the stairs.

'Enjoy your lunch!' Sean called after him mischievously

Sean and I were back on board by 1.30. Leading by example was something I prided myself in. It also gave me some time before I had to be skipper again.

While we were eating lunch, the police had called with an update. Hugo was still in a medically-induced coma, but they told us the doctors were hopeful it would only be for another three or four days, which was great news. They did explain though, that even when Hugo did wake up, he might not remember anything straight away. The attack on Hugo consumed my thoughts, but we had to continue with our journey.

'We're setting sail for St Lucia this evening. If I give you the sat phone number, would you please keep us updated?'

'Of course, señora.'

'Did you manage to speak to this Mateo person? The one Liliana told us about?'

'Sí, señora. He confessed to hitting Señorita Liliana, but he was not in the marina when your friend was hurt. We have a video of him somewhere else.' The policeman went on to explain that while Mateo had been looking for Hugo, he was not looking in the right place; Liliana had sent him off in the wrong direction.

With the exception of Danny, the rest of the crew returned to *Duchess* in plenty of time. Danny strolled along the jetty ten minutes late, in what I was certain was a calculated move. He knew I would look petty if I became annoyed over such a minor thing; this was his way of showing I wasn't the boss of him. He was trying to let me know who was really in charge.

A couple of hours later, we were ready to sail out of the marina and into the rolling swell of the Atlantic.

The crew was on deck, just as I liked it. Although I wasn't one for superstitions, this made me happy and I somehow got away with it by labelling it a tradition; something happy and to look forward to. Knowing everyone was here and accounted for, relaxed me for the first part of any voyage.

I did a final count up and realised not everyone was on deck. Of *course* Danny was still down below; just another way for him to push back.

'Jonty, could you pop down and give Danny a nudge, please.' I hoped my words were light-hearted; just an oversight on Danny's part, nothing to worry about. Inside, I was grateful it was Jonty who was closest to the hatch.

'He says he'll be up in a minute and not to wait for him.' Jonty's words were even, his eyes told me a different story.

Enough was enough. Time for me to remind my son who was captain around here, even if that was just for show in his case. I made my way down the stairs calmly, for the benefit of the rest of the crew, and opened the door of Danny's cabin. He was lying on the top bunk, scrolling on his phone.

'Danny, we're setting sail in a minute, can you come up top with everyone else, please?'

'I told Jonty I'd be up in a minute.' He didn't look at me.

'I know that, but we're leaving now. I agreed to your terms, but I am still the skipper—'

'That's right, you did.' His voice was light enough, but the menace was there. 'I *could* always tell your friends…'

'You could, but you don't want them finding out either. I'm trying to help you and if I don't make you join us for the sail away, they're going to know something's up. You'll only be up there for half an hour anyway, then you can do whatever you want until your first watch.'

Danny stared at me for a few moments and I watched his decision-making process play out across his face; I knew his expressions well. I refused to break eye contact.

'Fine.' He swung his legs around so quickly I had to take a step back.

I made my way up the stairs, a fake smile fixed on my face. 'Right, shall we get going then?'

Connor and Sean released the lines fore and aft and I steered

Duchess out into the middle of the marina. As we approached the mouth of the harbour I called for the sails to be unfurled and turned off the engines.

After a little bit of grinding in the ropes, adjusting the sails and checking our course, I could relax. We were on our way.

CHAPTER SEVENTEEN

THE NORTH ATLANTIC – DAY THREE

Our first days at sea passed by without incident. They were the long and boring days that meant we were safe and things are going well, but with such a long passage, sailors often wish for *something* to happen. Something nice, like dolphins or other sea creatures, bioluminescence or shooting stars. No one dared say anything though for fear of manifesting a storm, or something much worse.

The crew settled down, and although people rarely spoke to Danny, they were at least civil, as Danny was to them. I started to think maybe things wouldn't be so bad after all.

It didn't last for long.

On the third day of our voyage, I woke with the sun streaming through my window. Sunrise happened early in the Atlantic, so I couldn't be sure what time it was. I checked my watch and remembered we were due to turn our time back at midnight, which meant it was only 6.30am. Turning the time back by one hour while travelling west was a trick I'd picked up from an old skipper years ago. It meant when we arrived we would be less jet-lagged. It worked even better heading east and advancing time.

Flick was on forenoon watch, which meant she was already up and I was alone in the cabin. I snuggled under the blankets and decided to allow myself the luxury of a lie-in. Someone would call if they needed me. Today was my day off and I planned to relax as much as possible. I was going to try and let everyone do their jobs without me interfering. They were perfectly capable and me hovering and constantly checking up on them would only add to the tension.

I knew what they thought of me. That I was too strict, too *uptight*, that I needed to let things go occasionally. Somehow I couldn't explain to them the responsibility I felt. Not just for *Duchess*, but for them as well. If I *let something go* and anything happened to a member of my crew, or the boat, I would never forgive myself. And not just because it could cost me in my pocket. And not because a dereliction of duty could see me in prison.

It went further than that. I felt a moral responsibility for my crew and the yacht. The owner had entrusted an incredibly expensive possession to me and the crew, most of whom were friends and had, essentially, entrusted me with their lives. They were trusting me to keep them safe and it was a confidence I would do everything in my power not to lose.

Despite all of that, I was sick of being the bad guy. So today, I would take a back seat, maybe even read a book. The charts were all there for everyone to look at, and with the exception of Erin, they could all read them if they needed or wanted to. But the route was in the plotter in the cockpit and would tell them exactly which course they needed to follow. I might even sunbathe on the foredeck now things were getting brighter, if the wind wasn't too high.

By 7.30 I hadn't gone back to sleep and I was bored. How did people sit around and do *nothing* all the time? In the saloon I could hear Nick and Flick mumbling quietly to one another. No doubt Erin would be up as well. Given how little sleep she seemed to get, I was constantly surprised at how she managed to keep going.

After dressing, I took my wash bag to the heads, brushed my teeth and had a quick wash. Back in the saloon someone had made me a cup of coffee and I sank into the sofa to take a sip, grateful for the forethought.

'Everything all right, Helen?'

I looked up. 'Everything's fine, why?'

There was a lot of exchanging of looks. I frowned.

'You just normally sit at the chart table, Mum, that's all,' Connor said.

'Oh, yeah, well I'm quite happy with them to be honest. This is much more comfortable, isn't it?' I gave the sofa cushions a squeeze. They were still staring at me. I rolled my eyes. 'I'm going to sit in the cockpit and enjoy the morning sun.'

'Morning, Helen. Everything okay?' Sean asked from behind the wheel as I climbed onto the deck and settled myself on one of the cockpit benches.

'Good morning. Yeah, everything's fine. Just going to enjoy some sunshine with my coffee for a little while.'

Sean raised an eyebrow, but didn't say any more.

Five minutes later Nick and Flick arrived to take over watch, followed by Erin. Bella and Sean disappeared down below, no doubt for breakfast and coffee.

Erin sat opposite me, nursing her own drink and stared out to the horizon. I understood. It was calming, easy to get lost in your thoughts and time passed without you realising.

'How are you getting on?' I asked her. We'd settled into a slightly uneasy truce after Erin shouted at me before we left Gran Canaria. She'd made it clear she didn't want to talk about it, but I sensed she still seethed with anger.

'I'm okay, feeling much less queasy.'

The Atlantic could be like a rollercoaster ride at a theme park, except there was no way off, no way to make it stop. I'd seen more experienced sailors than Erin lose their stomachs over the side on the first few days of a crossing.

'Have you managed to keep anything down?'

Erin nodded, gesturing towards me with her cup.

'I meant food.'

'Yes, I've kept food down,' she snapped.

'I–'

'Sorry, I shouldn't have bitten your head off.' Erin rubbed at her forehead, an apparently apologetic gesture, but her words still stung.

'I know this is a lot. You can talk to me though, or anyone else if you'd prefer. We've all been there and we all have different ways of coping with the days. You'll find your way too.'

'Thanks, but I don't think talking about this is going to help.' She gave me a tight smile that told me she appreciated the effort, but she'd rather shit in her hands and clap.

That afternoon I convinced myself the weather was good enough and the sea was calm enough for me to sunbathe on the foredeck with my book. I lay on my towel, sunglasses on and a cushion behind my head. I'd read a few pages and then get distracted by the sea. It never changed, yet somehow the view was always fresh and vibrant.

I was mid-distraction when I heard a shout. I turned to look at Jonty and Danny behind me. Both looked alarmed and Jonty was waving at me frantically, calling my name. I stood up quickly, picking up my things, and made my way to the cockpit over the ropes and bits of hardware as quickly as I could without tripping.

'I can hear shouting down below,' Jonty said as I approached the cockpit.

I slid back the hatch and climbed down the steps. Nothing could have prepared me for the chaos I encountered.

Bella was slumped in the corner of the sofa; she looked like she was struggling to breathe. Erin was sitting beside her holding her hand. The rest of the crew were frantic: opening cupboards and drawers, calling out instructions and commentary.

'It's not here!'

'I can't find it!'

'Has anyone checked the heads?'

'What's happened?' I couldn't keep the panic from my voice, even though I didn't fully understand the emergency. I sat down on the other side of Bella and grasped her other hand.

'I think she's having an allergic reaction.' Erin looked terrified.

I tore my eyes from Bella's face and looked at the cup in front of her. White coffee.

'Did you drink this?' I asked her, pointing at the cup.

Bella nodded, the wheezing getting even worse and I knew in that moment, in my heart, we were facing the worst possible ending.

'We need to find that EpiPen – now!' It was suddenly clear what everyone was searching for. 'It should be in the first aid kit. I put it there myself.'

'We've looked. It's not there.' Flick was close to tears.

'What do you mean?' I stood abruptly and pushed my way towards the cupboard with the medical supplies. Inside was a mess where someone had already searched. I forced myself to be slow, and I methodically pulled out each item, double-checking for Bella's EpiPen. The EpiPen I *knew* I'd put there myself; this was one of the reasons why I took control of the medical supplies – I only trusted myself to be sure.

Behind me I could hear things being thrown and dropped as the frantic search continued. I turned back to Bella and forced calm into my voice. 'Bella, I know this is really hard, but did you move your EpiPen?'

She shook her head, gasping.

'Do you have another one?'

Again she shook her head.

'FUCK!' A thought struck me and I dashed up the stairs.

'Danny! Please tell me you brought an EpiPen with you?' I shouted above the wind and sea.

'Of course I di–'

'We need it. For Bella!'

Danny jumped down the stairs in one leap.

'What's happening?' Jonty asked.

'No time!'

Back down below, Danny was rummaging in his bunk space, opening and closing compartments.

'For fuck sake! Hurry up!'

Danny growled, but he couldn't see Bella and I could. Her eyes were half-closed, as she slumped against Erin; her breathing becoming more and more shallow. She was close to losing consciousness and I knew if that happened, it was game over.

'Here.'

I snatched the pen from Danny's hand and rushed to Bella's side. Adrenaline was causing my hands to shake and I struggled to uncap the pen.

Danny ripped the pen from my hands. 'Get out of the way.'

He shoved me aside, pulled off the blue lid and then jammed the needle end hard into Bella's thigh, holding it there for a few seconds.

'What now? Will she be okay?' Erin was still panicking and her knuckles were white where she grasped Bella's hand.

'Hopefully.'

There was silence as we watched Bella's breathing settle back into something resembling normal. I prayed this one shot of epinephrine would be enough. It had to be: it was all we had.

I could physically feel the tension reduce as Bella's symptoms abated. There were rushes of air as, one by one, we all expelled our panic. The worry, however, remained.

I sat back down next to Bella. 'How are you feeling?'

'Okay. Tired.'

I wasn't surprised; I was exhausted and it wasn't me who'd had an allergic reaction.

We were surrounded by worried and anxious faces, which would be of no use to Bella. Time to be a captain again.

'Danny, you better get back to watch and can you fill Jonty in, please. Sean, can you help me get Bella into her bunk? The rest of you, can you tidy everything up, please?'

Erin was still holding Bella's hand and I wondered if she might be in shock. 'Erin, can you help tidy up, please?' I had no doubt she was having some kind of flashback, but now was not the time to be pandering. I was already a crew member down and I needed her to snap out of it. 'Erin!'

'Wha–? Oh, yeah, sure.'

Between us, Sean and I manoeuvred Bella around the table and helped her into her cabin. I shoved the detritus from the search onto Erin's side of the bed and we helped Bella climb up onto the bunk. She lay down and almost immediately fell asleep.

'I'll sit with her for a while. Can you bring me my water bottle and my book, please?'

'Sure.' Sean closed the door gently behind him. A minute or so later he was back with the items I had requested.

'Could you ask Erin to give us some space for a bit, please? I don't want anyone disturbing Bella. Oh, and you might need to organise watch cover, I'm not sure.'

'Leave it with me. I'll get it sorted. I'll check on you both in a couple of hours.' Sean turned to leave and then stopped, turning back to speak to me. 'Do we know what it was?'

'Bella's allergic to milk and there was a white coffee in front of her. It doesn't make any sense though; she's always taken her coffee black, just in case.'

CHAPTER EIGHTEEN

I sat with Bella for a couple of hours. At first I watched her sleep, constantly checking the rise and fall of her chest.

The missing EpiPen churned over in my mind. I saw her, again and again, handing it to me and me placing it with the rest of the medical supplies. I don't think I could have imagined it, but if I hadn't put it in the cupboard, where the bloody hell was it? At least two people searched that entire cupboard and didn't find it. Where had it gone? I couldn't imagine it falling out: the cupboards on board were designed to stop that. Which only left me with one thought and it was one I didn't want to look at too closely. Someone moved it.

Later, more confident Bella wasn't going to suddenly stop breathing on me and having driven myself half-mad with my ouroboros thoughts, I picked up my book and read for a while.

Eventually, Bella began to stir and I watched the tell-tale signs she was waking up. She groaned and turned over, her eyes opening slowly.

'Hey, how are you doing?' I asked softly, moving a piece of hair away from her face.

'Eugh.' She tried to sit up.

'Take it easy. Let me help you.'

Once she was in a sitting position, Bella scrubbed at her face and then said, 'I feel like I've been hit by a bus.'

'Do you remember what happened?'

'Sort of. I know I went into anaphylactic shock. Do I remember no one could find my EpiPen?' She looked at me, one eye screwed shut as she tried to recall.

'Yeah. It wasn't in the medical cupboard, but I know I put it in there. I remembered Danny should have one and we used his. Thank God he was here.' The ramifications of what might have happened if he hadn't been hit me with a thud.

'Yeah.' I could see Bella was thinking the same thing. She laid a hand on my arm. 'I saw you put my EpiPen in the cupboard. Don't go second-guessing yourself.'

I placed my hand on top of hers in acknowledgement. 'What possessed you to drink a white coffee anyway?'

Bella shook her head. 'I wasn't looking. I could have sworn someone said it was mine when it was put down in front of me. I was chatting to Nick, so I just picked it up and drank it.'

'Who–' But before I could finish there was a knock and the door opened a little. Erin's face appeared in the gap.

'Sorry, I heard voices and I wanted to see if you were okay?'

'I'll live,' said Bella with a small smile. The usually light-hearted, throwaway statement took a new and more sinister meaning.

'I'll get out of your hair for a bit. Erin, I'm sorry, but we had to shift everything out of the way to get Bella onto the bed.'

'It's fine, I'll have a tidy up.'

'I'm going to see if I can get hold of a doctor or someone on the sat phone. I want to check if there's anything we can do to make you feel better.' Bella would probably be okay, but I needed to be certain and this felt like a practical, useful thing to do.

'You can tell them I have steroids with me and antihistamines – prescribed ones. I'm pretty sure I know what I should be taking, but it's worth double-checking if you do get a hold of someone.'

I nodded and left their cabin, reciting the names of the medications Bella had given me in my head. Outside, in the saloon, I sank onto the sofa and leant forward, my elbows on my knees. I closed my eyes and took three long, deep breaths.

Feeling calmer, I was ready to resume my responsibilities and I would start by contacting Falmouth Coastguard to patch me through to a medic. I retrieved the sat phone from its cupboard and made my way up on deck.

Falmouth answered virtually straight away and told me they would find the on-call doctor and phone me back. Twenty minutes later I was speaking to the doctor.

By this time though, the signal was intermittent at best and the call kept dropping out. It took three attempts for me to explain where we were and that we had already administered the EpiPen, and that I was looking for advice going forward.

After some back and forth, I was finally given some instructions to relay to Bella. The upshot of it all was that she should take her steroids as prescribed and rest for as long as she needed. I signed off after promising faithfully that I would ensure Bella was seen by a doctor when we arrived in St Lucia. Personally, I wasn't sure there would be much point by the time we got there, but I wasn't the expert or the person with a potentially life-threatening allergy.

I didn't even entertain the notion of turning round – I just couldn't allow it to happen.

After stowing the sat phone, I relayed the doctor's message to Bella who wasn't at all surprised and asked me to get her some water.

Back at my chart table, where people rarely interrupted me, I couldn't help but think over what had happened. Everyone *knew* Bella had a milk allergy: we covered it in our very first briefing. Had I not stressed the point enough? Had I not made everyone aware of the consequences? Told everyone where to find the EpiPen? I was certain I had made it clear this was a life and death matter, but maybe it needed even more?

A thought struck me.

'Who gave Bella the coffee with milk in it?' I said it to myself and then repeated more loudly. 'Guys, who gave Bella the coffee with milk in it?'

There were blank looks all round.

'Sean, who was here?'

'Um, me, Nick, Bella, Erin... The others were in their cabins, I think, and came out when they heard shouting.'

'Erin, can you come here for a second, please?' I raised my voice so she could hear me through the closed door.

There was some shuffling and then the cabin door opened. 'Did someone call me?' Erin asked, standing in the doorway.

'It was me; can you come and join us for a minute, please?'

'Sure.' Erin slid onto the end of the sofa nearest her.

'I was just trying to figure out who gave Bella the milky coffee?'

Erin looked around, wide-eyed. 'I-I don't know.'

'I made the coffees,' said Sean, 'but I'm sure I made a black one. I looked afterwards though, and all the cups had milk in them. Oh God, maybe it was me?' Sean's eyes grew wide as the ramifications hit him.

'Where are the cups now?' I asked.

'I poured them away. I'm sorry, I thought I was being helpful by tidying up.' Erin smiled unhappily.

Sean was crying now and my heart went out to him; Nick put an arm around him and pulled him into a half hug.

'Sean, it was an accident. It's not like you meant to hurt her.

Did you?' I made sure the final words were said with a smile, and a levity I didn't feel, to try and lighten the mood.

'Look mate, she's fine now. Or she will be after some rest. It was an accident and I know you're going to be double- and triple-checking everything from now on, aren't you?' I was grateful to Nick for trying to reassure Sean as well.

'Too fucking right!' Sean would be angry at himself for a while, I knew.

'The other question is, where the hell was Bella's EpiPen?' Flick asked.

No one said anything.

'I've been thinking about that too. I know I put it in the cupboard and Bella confirmed she saw me do it.' I shrugged, hoping someone would give me a reasonable solution.

'I just don't know why anyone would even be in there. We haven't needed anything in that cupboard the whole trip.'

'Maybe it was because a certain person wanted to look like a hero,' Erin volunteered and I was shocked when all eyes turned to me.

'What? You can't–'

'It's obvious isn't it? Danny is literally the only person who could save the day.'

The full meaning behind Erin's words washed over me, slowly at first, until the full ramifications of what she was saying thudded into my chest.

'Don't be ridiculous, Erin, Danny wasn't even down here. And besides, I can't imagine someone who actually carries an EpiPen ever doing anything to cause someone else to need one.' Nick spoke quickly, recognising the signs of my temper about to explode.

'*Anyone* could've taken that pen, or moved it by mistake without thinking.' I spoke softly, dangerously.

Jonty spoke for the first time. 'I just don't see how.'

'I think I need some air.' Erin stood and made her way to the stairs and up onto the deck.

'What's got into her?' Flick asked.

'Dunno,' Nick said. He and Sean shook their heads.

Whatever passes I had given Erin since Rhea died suddenly expired.

CHAPTER NINETEEN

I suppose I should have seen it coming. Given their personality types, it was only a matter of time before they buddied up. I wasn't happy about it; there was no doubt they would be a bad influence on one another. There had already been too much drama, and I could do without any cliques forming before we arrived in St Lucia.

Carl and Danny became inseparable. In the daytime they would sit with one another during their watches and when they were off together, they could be found sitting on the foredeck, their heads close, chatting constantly.

Erin and I were lounging in the cockpit; Nick and Flick were on watch. After a lot of thought, I'd come to the conclusion there was no point in confronting her about what she'd said about Danny. There just wasn't enough room on *Duchess* for that sort of argument, and apart from anything else, I needed to set an example. I stored it in a room of its own in my mind, where I could find it later if I wanted to.

'I really wish those two didn't get along so well,' I said.

'Where's the harm? It could be worse, they could hate each other and argue all the time,' Erin replied.

'True. I just don't trust them. They're up to something, I'm sure of it.'

Erin snorted. 'What could they possibly be up to? We're the only boat for miles around, and if they *are* planning anything untoward, they can't do anything about it until they're off the boat.'

'I wouldn't be so sure. My son has an uncanny ability to create problems in an empty room, as you well know.' I arched an eyebrow letting her know I didn't think for one second my son was a saint. 'And for all intents and purposes, this is an empty room.'

'I think you're worrying too much.'

I was a little surprised at Erin's complete 180 on Danny, but maybe this was her way of apologising. 'I know my son, and I know the kinds of things he's done in the past. Trust me on this one.'

Erin nodded in agreement, but she really didn't know the half of it.

I pulled my eyes away from the two boys, men I suppose, and caught Erin giving me a funny look. I sighed. 'Maybe you're right, but I don't trust either of them. Just… if you hear anything funny, let me know?'

'Like what?'

'I don't know!' I removed my cap, flattened my hair, and replaced it, pulling it down firmly. 'Just…' I shrugged, palms turned up.

'Okay, fine, I'll let you know if I hear them planning to set fire to the boat or something.' Erin was flippant, rolling her eyes. I hardened my stare. 'Okay, okay! I'll let you know if I do, but I really think you're reading too much into it.'

'I hope you're right,' I said, sipping my water.

Later that day, we were eating dinner around the table in the saloon when the subject of the extra cabin came up.

'What's the deal with the skipper's cabin anyway?' Erin asked.

'Why do you ask?' Danny stared.

'Just curious.' Erin shrugged.

'It's like I told you before, sometimes a chartered boat needs a skipper, and when the cabins are full that's where the skipper sleeps. It also gives the skipper some privacy away from clients when they need it.'

'And Christ do they need it sometimes,' joked Sean.

After that we told our horror stories, including my personal favourite of a client who spent the entire time drunk, but refused to be strapped to the boat during a particularly windy spell. We managed to save him from going in twice, but the third time we were too late and experienced a completely horrendous, and not to mention unnecessary, man-overboard situation. Oddly enough, after that, he did as he was told.

'There's no way you'd get me sleeping in there,' Erin said with a shudder. 'Actually, you wouldn't even get me in there full stop. The thought of being in there with the window – door, whatever it is – shut, makes my skin crawl.'

'It's not so bad,' Nick replied. 'You do get used to it after a while.'

'Maybe, but when the only way in and out is in the ceiling, it gives me the heebie-jeebies.'

'No one's using it for this trip anyway though, are they?' Danny asked.

'No,' I said quickly. 'We've got some supplies stored in there, but that's about it.'

Danny nodded and glanced at Carl.

'Could you imagine being trapped in there and the boat starts to sink? I couldn't think of anything worse.' Erin was overthinking things.

'Being burned alive. That's worse.'

'It's not a competition, Carl,' I said above everyone else's cries of disgust.

'Yeah, let's not do that,' Sean said, his voice laced with revulsion.

'She brought it up,' Carl replied and laughed.

'Let's talk about something else, shall we?' I tried to change the subject.

'I take it you don't have any news about Hugo?' Bella asked.

Hugo. I hadn't thought about him for a while, and for a moment I felt guilty. How could I have forgotten about Hugo? The clunk of cutlery against plates stilled and I became acutely aware Bella was not the only one waiting for an answer. With difficulty I swallowed the food I'd not yet finished chewing.

'No, nothing yet. I don't suppose we'll hear anything until we get there now.'

After that, everyone seemed content to eat in silence and I made no attempt to restart the conversation.

The following day the weather was unusually terrible when we woke up. November and December are considered two of the best months for sailing the Atlantic: any kind of foul weather is an anomaly.

Bella and Sean came off the morning watch wet through and looking utterly miserable. Nick and Flick did not look any happier at the prospect of having to go and sit in it for the next four hours. When you're sailing across the Atlantic towards the sun and warmth, the last thing you want to be doing is sitting in the rain and wind with your foul-weather gear on. I offered a silent prayer to Neptune to clear the inclement weather before it was mine and Erin's turn in a few hours.

'I think it's best we all stay below until this front clears out. I don't want anyone getting ill and I really don't want anyone ending up overboard.'

I was rewarded with a chorus of grumbling.

'I know, I know, but it's not like it's forever. Does anyone really want to be sitting out in that anyway? Let's just chill out, make use of the space we do have, and hope it clears up soon.'

'I was going to get some bits from the skipper's cabin for lunch,' Connor said.

'I'll go,' Danny replied. Everyone stared; it wasn't like him to volunteer for anything. 'What? I'm just trying to be helpful.'

As my head turned back towards Connor, my eyes stayed with Danny for a few seconds. 'No one is going to the skipper's cabin for the moment. Connor, can you rustle something up with what we've got here?'

'Um...' Connor opened the fridge and stared at the contents. 'Yeah... I probably can actually.'

'Okay, let's do that. It'll be a good exercise in using up leftovers too.'

Later that afternoon, people were beginning to get fractious. Jonty and Flick had been bickering non-stop for almost twenty minutes when Danny lost his temper and told them to pack it in. Flick stormed off into our bunk and slammed the door behind her.

'Now look what you've done,' Jonty snapped.

'What *I've* done? You're the one who's been arguing with her all afternoon,' Danny retorted. Suddenly there were two grown men squaring off against one another in a tiny space.

'That's enough!' I roared. 'You're all as bad as each other. Go to your cabins and cool off. Anyone else with excess energy can clean.'

The crew took my suggestion and embarked on a cleaning frenzy. Before long everywhere was spotless and the atmosphere inside had cooled down to congenial. Afterwards, books and magazines were read, card games were played, and Nick and Flick on watch had drunk more than their fill of warm drinks.

Soon after, I felt the boat calm in the water and someone shouted they could see blue sky through a porthole. We scrambled towards the stairs, eager to be out in the fresh air and sunshine. The hatch was pushed back and one by one we made our way on deck, sunglasses and caps already in place.

Pleased, I let them all dash off in front of me, before joining them. I was as relieved as they were, but I couldn't help wonder how they would cope if we ended up in the middle of a storm. It was rare at this time of year, but it could happen. I crossed my fingers and prayed to Neptune *and* Poseidon – just to be on the safe side – that we would have sunshine for the rest of the journey.

Connor was keeping a close eye on the weather and downloading data every so often, and so far everything looked good.

We laid out the wet foul-weather gear to dry in the late afternoon sun, and then Erin and I took over watch for a couple of hours.

CHAPTER TWENTY

THE NORTH ATLANTIC – DAY EIGHT

Bang! Bang! Bang!

I was barely even awake as I sat upright, my heart thumping in my throat. A few seconds later I slumped back down onto my pillow and took some deep breaths. It was just someone knocking on my cabin door. The dream I'd been having had seemed so real...

I rolled over, checked the time and groaned. I'd only come off middle watch at 4am and by the time I'd got to bed it was almost 4.30. Whoever it was banging on my door at seven had better have a bloody good reason; like the boat was sinking.

'What?' I called, refusing to get up in case there was any chance I could get some more sleep.

I heard the door open and opened one eye to see who it was.

'Mum, are you awake?'

'For God sake, Connor. I was on middle, what the hell do you want?'

'I need to talk to you.'

'Can it not wait until I've slept? I'm back on at midday.'

'I found something.'

'What do you mean, you found something?'

'In the skipper's cabin.'

His words chased any further thoughts of sleep from my mind and I was suddenly alert. I sat up again and looked at him properly. 'What were you doing in there?'

'We needed more supplies, I told you that yesterday.' Connor was indignant and he had a right to be. The skipper's cabin wasn't out of bounds.

'Sorry,' I said, making a show of rubbing the sleep from my face. 'I'm still half asleep. What did you find?'

'I need to show you.'

I swallowed hard, glad he couldn't see me properly in the gloom. 'Really? Can you not just tell me?'

Connor shook his head, his lips pressed firmly shut. He looked worried.

'Ugh, fine. Let me put some clothes on first.' I shooed him out the door and then threw back the covers.

A few minutes later we were standing on the foredeck and Connor pulled open the skylight entrance. Nerves fizzed in my stomach. We climbed down inside and shut the window; the waves were too high for it to be left open.

'Right, what is it you're so desperate to show me that couldn't wait until I woke up.' I asked the question, but I was delaying the inevitable. I knew exactly what he was going to show me.

The skipper's cabin was tiny and every available space was made use of; the people who came up with these space-saving solutions were geniuses. There wasn't really enough room for two people, but I hadn't been given a lot of choice in the matter.

Connor bent down and began to rummage around near the toilet, which was partially covered by a folding wooden panel; when the head was in use, the panel sat upright and when the bed was in use, it folded down. Since neither the bed nor the toilet were required for this journey, there were all sorts of supplies stacked on the bed and strapped down.

There wasn't a lot of room in the space behind the toilet and under the folding panel, but I knew, as soon as Connor made for that part of the cabin, we were busted.

When he stood upright he was holding a brown paper package about the size of a house brick. He turned and offered it to me. I didn't take it, forcing my hands to remain by my sides.

'What's that?'

'I don't know for certain, but I could have a guess.'

I tried to keep my expression neutral and breathe normally. 'Oh?'

'You don't have any idea what this might be?'

I pulled, what I hoped was, a doubtful look and shook my head. 'No, I don't.'

'Oh for God sake, Mum! It's drugs! There are about ten of these stuffed under here, and that's just the ones I've found.'

'I don't understand?' There was a reason I'd never made it as an actor.

'What is there to understand? Someone has brought drugs on board and I've a pretty good idea who.'

I gave him my best blank look.

'Danny!'

'I don't think–'

'Don't. Don't defend him, if it wasn't Danny, then who else?'

I pretended to think for a moment. 'Carl?' I offered, weakly.

Connor scoffed at me and threw the package down. 'For fuck sake, Mum!'

I leaned back, startled. Connor rarely swore, and I didn't think he had ever sworn at *me*. His whole face was tense, his eyes scowling. I was used to this behaviour from Danny, but angry Connor was alien to me.

'Say something then.' His voice was loud in the small space, already over-occupied with us both in there.

I struggled to think of words. He was right of course, the drugs did belong to Danny and I knew all about them. Only, I didn't want Connor to know that. Smuggling the drugs on board

Duchess was what Danny asked of me. Connor and I had never discussed what Danny did for a living, and I was pretty sure I only knew the half of it.

'Fine.' Connor pushed open the skylight, letting it bang on the deck, and climbed out. He moved so quickly, by the time I realised what he was doing, all I could see were his disappearing feet.

'Connor, wait!'

Shit!

I scrambled out after him, closing the window behind me. I tried calling his name again, but the wind snatched my words. Nick and Flick were staring at me from the cockpit, and Nick was pointing towards the hatch.

Fuck!

As I neared the cockpit, Flick called out to me. 'Everything okay? Connor looked furious.'

I held my hand up and shook my head. I didn't have time to explain right now and neither did I want to.

Down below, Connor had the door to his and Danny's bunk space open and was demanding his brother get out of bed.

'Connor, I–'

'No, Mum, I want to know what the fuck he thinks he's doing. Get your arse out here and explain.'

Connor's shouts had brought everyone else into the saloon. Their questioning looks switching between us, and our apparent family argument, and each other.

'What's going on?' Bella asked.

Heads were shook and shoulders were shrugged. The only people who knew exactly what was going on weren't about to answer.

'Can you please shut the door so I can put some clothes on? I don't think everyone wants to see me in all my glory.' Danny's voice was calm as he gestured to the room.

Connor slammed the door and tried to pace up and down the

gap between the dining table and the galley. People scrambled and stumbled to get out of his way, but even so, there wasn't enough room for more than five or six steps.

After ten trips up and down the walkway, Danny emerged from his cabin. Connor faced him, his features contorted into pure hatred.

I wanted to tell everyone to go up on deck, or go back to their cabins, but there wasn't any point. They would find out; it might be for the best.

'What's going on?' Danny was unruffled. I was reluctantly impressed; he *must* have known why Connor was so angry.

'Why don't you tell us? I've just been in the skipper's cabin to get some supplies. After your reaction yesterday, I thought I'd have a poke around.'

'Did you now?' Danny's face was stony, his voice dangerously calm.

'Yeah, I did and guess what I found?'

There wasn't a breath in the room. All eyes were on Danny, waiting for his answer. Danny's eyes were black and fixed on Connor, his mouth blank.

I could see Connor getting more and more worked up the longer Danny refused to answer his question. I waited for the inevitable explosion.

'Drugs!'

I closed my eyes. I didn't want to see the shock and astonishment on their faces. This was it; this was the turning point. After trying so hard to keep everyone balanced, we had fallen off the side and the rest of our journey was going to be fractious. It couldn't not be.

Then Danny spoke and it got worse. 'Why don't you ask Mum? She knows all about it.'

CHAPTER TWENTY-ONE

S even pairs of eyes turned to look at me, like ventriloquist's dummies. Had the whole situation not been so serious I might've laughed. It looked like something from a bad thriller film.

'Helen?' Jonty was the first to speak.

I looked from him to Danny, to Connor and then caught Carl's eye. He knew – of course he did. That's what he and Danny had been talking about the whole time. Had he always known?

'You knew?' Connor's anger drained from his body and disappointment replaced it.

I sighed. 'Thanks for that, Danny.'

His smile in return was smug.

I sat down in my usual place at the chart table and wondered how I was going to explain. How could I make them understand why I had allowed drugs to be smuggled on my boat? I rubbed the bridge of my nose, my eyes closed to shut everyone out and give myself a moment.

How much of the truth should I tell them?

Do I tell them the whole truth? That if Danny couldn't transport the supply to the Caribbean then his life was in danger?

That I had no choice, as his mother, but to help and protect him? That in helping him I was also helping myself?

Judging by the look on everyone else's faces, their opinion of me couldn't get much lower. This was partly Danny's mess and I wasn't about to go down by myself.

'Yes, I did know about it.' I looked up, gauging their reaction, but continued before they could interrupt. 'I do have my reasons though.'

'They better be fucking good ones,' Jonty said.

'Let her speak, Jonty.' Erin glared at me, making sure there was no mistake. She wasn't defending me, she wanted to know.

'Danny needed my help.'

'Mum.' Danny was warning me. I ignored him.

'He got himself in with some nasty people, violent people, and needed my help to transport the drugs across the Atlantic. He wasn't given an option, which meant I wasn't given an option. I'm his mother, I *had* to help him.'

'Don't forget your part,' Danny said gruffly. He wasn't going down by himself either.

'Also, I, uh, I panicked when we found out Hugo was in hospital and wouldn't be able to crew with us. Danny was the only person I knew of who was experienced enough and would be available at such short notice.'

'We could have looked for someone else,' said Sean. 'We didn't even try. An extra day or two wouldn't have made much difference.' He was trying to understand, but I didn't blame him for being confused.

I cleared my throat unnecessarily and licked my lips. 'Apart from wanting to help Danny, I– um, I couldn't afford the delay. I…' Taking a deep breath, I prepared myself. This was it. 'The truth is, I'm in quite a bit of debt and the fee for this trip would pay off a chunk of it. If we'd waited another couple of days then the penalties would have caused me serious problems.'

'Why not just explain to the bank? They're pretty

understanding these days as long as you speak to them. Haven't you got some kind of payment plan?' Bless Bella for trying to understand, for trying to be the voice of calm amongst people whose respect I had lost in a matter of minutes.

I closed my eyes and swallowed hard before I spoke. 'My loan isn't with a bank.'

Silence.

When I opened my eyes, my crew were exchanging looks with each other, clearly confused. Only my sons looked at me. One knew for sure, because I'd told him when I called. The other though, looked as though he'd guessed.

'Who?' It was Connor.

'Malky McFadyen,' I whispered.

'Big Malky McFadyen?' Connor asked, his eyes wide.

I nodded.

'For fuck sake, Mum!' Connor said angrily.

I could feel tears threatening and I didn't want anyone to think I was looking for sympathy, so I kept quiet and tried to breathe through it.

'But why?' His tone was softer now he'd had a minute to process what I'd said and what that meant.

Big Malky McFadyen was what we called a nasty bastard. Being a woman meant nothing. If I couldn't pay what I owed, with eye-watering amounts of interest, then he'd send his boys round, just the same. This whole trip was about helping myself *and* helping my son.

I sat up straight, cleared my throat. There was no point in shying away now. 'I have a gambling addiction. It got out of control about a year ago and I couldn't afford to pay the mortgage. I went to Malky for a short-term loan to tide me over. Except I didn't stop gambling and I did keep losing. And, of course, the interest kept going up.'

'Why didn't you tell me, Mum?'

'Because it's not your problem, it's mine and I didn't want you to worry.'

'But I could've helped.'

'Yeah, like what you earn could make any kind of a dent in what she owes,' Danny scoffed.

'How much do you–'

I cut Connor off, knowing what his question would be. 'Twenty-five grand last time his thugs came to see me.'

'Twenty-five grand! Jesus Christ, Mum!'

I stared at my hands and picked at the skin around my fingernails. I'd never felt so ashamed.

Connor had resumed pacing in the short gangway space. I felt his frustration at not being able to stretch out, at not having the space to rant, at having nowhere to go. All I wanted to do was hide away in my cabin until we reached St Lucia.

'What about now?'

'I don't–'

'Are you still gambling? How are you managing while we're at sea? Are you radioing in horse bets when there's no one around?' Contempt dripped from every word.

'No, of course not!' I checked myself and lowered my voice. 'I haven't placed a bet for over three months. I've been going to Gamblers Anonymous and being in the middle of nowhere with no signal certainly helps with the cravings.'

Everyone was silent and now I'd started, I felt compelled to finish my confession.

'I'm sorry, but I had no choice. They threatened to go after you two if I didn't get this payment to them by the time I said I would.'

'So, what's the plan then?' Erin spoke up.

'What do you mean?'

'When we get there, what's the plan? What happens if we get searched by customs? I'm telling you now, I'm sure as hell not taking the blame for–'

'You won't say a fucking word,' Danny growled, but I knew he was scared too.

'Danny! That's enough! They have a right to ask questions.' I jabbed a finger at him.

Erin looked frightened and I didn't blame her. Danny wasn't exactly small, and the daunting realisation that we were very much on our own could be overwhelming at times.

'Once we get nearer to St Lucia, a boat will come and meet us to take the drugs off our hands.'

'Mum!'

'They need to know, Danny. If *Duchess* is searched and the drugs are found, then we're all for it.'

'Right, but once they're off the boat, nobody can prove anything and everyone keeps their mouth shut, right?'

'Fuck off, Danny.' Connor standing up to his brother both surprised and pleased me. At least I'd brought up one of them right.

I was drained: mentally and physically exhausted, from a lack of sleep and from being forced to reveal our secrets. I had one more thing I needed to do though. 'Does anyone have any questions right now?'

Everyone shook their heads and there were murmurs of 'no'.

I stood and made my way up the stairs. Nick and Flick would be aware something was going on and they had a right to hear it from me.

CHAPTER TWENTY-TWO

Coming clean and explaining everything to Nick and Flick was equally as excruciating as it had been the first time around. Nick was one of my closest friends and I felt I'd let him down terribly.

Despite this, I grew irritated by the constant probing questions, mainly led by Erin who had joined us in the cockpit. I was drained, exhausted, and all I wanted to do was go to my cabin and try to sleep for an hour. My next watch was four hours long and although it was in the afternoon and there would be people up and about, I had a feeling I would be given a wide berth.

'So, how did you find out about Gamblers Anonymous? Is there one near you, or did you have to travel?' Erin's questions were becoming less and less relevant.

'Erin, I'm really sorry, but can we do this later? We were on morning watch and then Connor had me up before eight. I really need to try and get some rest before afternoon.' I watched as her face fell. 'I'm not surprised you're full of questions, and I will answer them, but perhaps we can do it when we're on watch?'

'Yeah, that's fine. Sorry, didn't mean to badger you.'

'It's okay. I'll catch up with you in a bit.' I stood and made my way below, not stopping to speak to, or look at, anyone. I lay down on my bed, and as I dropped my head onto the pillow a thought occurred to me. *I bet she's putting this in her bloody book!*

I dozed until it was time for my watch, unable to fall asleep properly as thoughts of loan sharks and drug dealers rolled around in my mind. I took over from Nick at the helm and Erin joined me soon after, handing me a cup of coffee. I braced myself for what I assumed would be a barrage of questions.

Erin settled herself at the table in the cockpit, and I'm almost certain I saw her fiddling with her mobile phone. I only saw her out of the corner of my eye and by the time I turned to look properly she was cradling her mug in both hands.

I wasn't about to start a conversation, but I wished she would. I didn't feel like I had a right to talk about anything *normal* and I couldn't think how to bring up drugs or debt without sounding defensive.

Eventually Erin spoke and when she asked her first question, I knew she wasn't asking as my friend or a member of my crew; she was asking as a writer.

'How did it all start?'

I stared into the distance for a moment, clenching my jaw against calling her out. If I'd looked her in the eye, she would've seen my irritation all too clearly. I'd told her I'd talk and after all I'd done, I didn't feel I could back out. In that moment I was darkly thankful Erin was a fiction writer, and not a reporter.

We talked for a couple of hours. As the time wore on, it became less like an interview and more like a conversation, for which I was grateful. However, despite wanting my watch to pass quickly, between Erin's interrogation and my lack of sleep, I was exhausted and I couldn't stand any more of her probing. I wasn't sure how to bring things to a natural end, so I opted for blunt instead.

'There's not really much more to tell you to be honest, and my brain needs a rest.'

'Oh, okay.' Erin took the hint and we passed the rest of the watch in silence. Unusually, but unsurprisingly, none of the rest of the crew came to spend any time with us.

By 6pm I had managed to get some sleep and was beginning to feel more human. Although I wanted nothing more than to eat by myself, I knew it wasn't a good look, so I forced myself to join the others around the table.

Conversation was strained and I didn't think it was my place to try and lighten the mood.

I realised I was gobbling at my food; trying to eat as quickly as possibly in order to escape to my cabin. I forced myself to slow down to a normal pace. No matter what I did, time slowed and then felt like it had come to a standstill.

I watched the others and as they ate, none of them looked at me. Not that I saw anyway. Danny was standing in the kitchen eating his food, a smirk plastered across his face. I wanted nothing more than to slap it off. Yes, I'd agreed to help him, but I despised him for putting me in this situation. For forcing me to lie to my friends, risk being arrested and thrown in prison, and now for enjoying every minute of everyone else's discomfort. Couldn't he just be a little bit more humble?

When I'd finally finished eating and everyone began to move around, I picked up my plate and took it to the galley. I tried to slip into my cabin unnoticed, but before I could even put my hand on the handle I heard my name.

'Helen?'

I turned. It was Bella who had spoken, but six people were looking at me. My stomach churned; I hated confrontation.

'What's up?' Stupid thing to say because it was pretty obvious what was up, but I didn't know what else to say.

'Can we talk to you, please?' Bella had clearly been voted spokesperson, and it appeared to be a role she was comfortable in.

'Of course.' I sat down at the chart table, it made me feel like I was still in charge, even if that were not strictly the case anymore. 'What do you want to talk about?' I already knew, but it seemed like the right thing to say at the time.

'It's about the... drugs.' Bella glanced towards Jonty who nodded his encouragement. 'We – and Nick and Flick are in agreement – don't think it's fair that our lives are at risk–'

Danny snorted, interrupting. 'It's not your lives that are at risk. This isn't some movie where the gangsters don't care who's collateral.'

'That's not what I meant,' Bella snapped. 'I mean if we're caught, this will ruin our lives, our livelihoods, even though it has nothing to do with us.'

I couldn't help but agree with her, but there wasn't a lot could be done about it now. Yes, I'd gone behind their backs and perhaps I would do things differently if given the chance again, but I couldn't figure out where she was going with this. I stayed silent and waited for her to continue.

'What we want is for the drugs to be removed from the boat.' She spoke quickly, the words tumbling over one another.

Removed from the boat? To where?

Danny clearly had similar thoughts. 'Where do you think I'm going to put them? In case you hadn't noticed, we're in the middle of the fucking Atlantic Ocean.'

Bella glanced once more at her teammates who all gave her encouraging nods. 'We think we should throw them overboard.'

Danny burst out laughing, but there was absolutely no humour in it. 'You can't be serious?'

'We are.' Jonty spoke up this time.

Danny stood from his position sprawled on the sofa and turned to face everyone. 'And what do you expect me to tell the man who owns the drugs when we arrive in St Lucia? Oh, I'm really sorry, but the other people on the boat weren't comfortable with there being drugs on board, so we threw them into the sea? How do you think that will go? Because let me tell you, my life *is* on the line if I don't deliver these drugs. And I will have absolutely no hesitation in handing over your names if it comes to it.'

CHAPTER TWENTY-THREE

No one said anything for a few moments. I assumed everyone was, like me, trying to process what Danny had just said.

Of course drug dealers were dangerous people, it was one of the reasons I had all but disowned my son. Having said that, maternal instinct wasn't something you could easily remove, no matter how hard you tried to kid yourself. I did not want him to die.

'Danny's right, they'll kill him if he doesn't deliver the drugs. If they don't, his boss will. Either way, his life is in danger and I will do what it takes to help him.' I stopped to take a breath and Danny jumped in.

'And I won't think twice about telling them what you did and giving them your names. They'll want payment for what was thrown away and for the money they've already spent transporting the drugs. As far as you're concerned, we're all in this together now.'

Worried looks were exchanged.

'So we really don't have any choice, but to hope we aren't caught?' Flick was angry.

'We won't get caught,' Danny said. 'I've told you: a boat will come and meet us before we get into port. A smaller boat that can land ashore in places where there are no customs or harbour police. You have nothing to worry about.'

'You'll forgive us if we don't have faith in the word of some druggie,' Jonty muttered.

Danny rounded on him, snarling. 'I am *not* a druggie. Don't you dare group me in with those pathetic losers.'

'I know this is pretty shit.' I needed to cool tempers. 'That I've done a really shitty thing, but you have to know, I would never have done it if we weren't desperate.'

'Was this all planned? Did you and Danny plan this together?' Realisation passed across Bella's face, but what she thought she realised, I couldn't say.

'What? No, of course not. Why would you think that?'

'You said it yourself, you need the money to pay back the loan shark. I assume you're getting a cut of the drug money?'

I exchanged a look with Danny. He shook his head very slightly, but being in a confined space meant very little was missed.

'I bloody knew it, you are, aren't you?' Bella was shouting.

'Hang on,' Jonty cut in, his face red. 'Was it you? Did you attack Hugo just so you could get on board?'

'Jesus Christ, it all makes sense now,' Bella said. 'Helen, how could you?'

'I-I-' I couldn't get the words out to defend myself.

'All that time you were pretending to be worried about Hugo, pretending not to know where he was, when you knew all along. You knew your animal of a son had attacked him, just so you could save your own skins.' Bella spat the words at me.

'No! That's not what happened. Tell them, Danny.'

'Mum's right, I didn't hurt Hugo and neither did Mum. Although, that would have been a pretty good plan; wish I'd thought of it.'

'So if that wasn't the plan, then how were you going to get the drugs to the Caribbean then?'

'There's always people looking for crew; I would've got there eventually. But when Mum called me, it seemed like too good an opportunity to pass up. We could help each other.'

'I would never intentionally hurt someone, not even to get my debts paid off. Surely you all know that?' I said desperately.

'To be honest, Helen, I didn't have you down as a drug smuggler either, but here we are. And to find out you're getting a pay-out from it too, well, you've got to admit, it all looks a bit dodgy.' Sean spoke for the first time. He seemed disgusted and disappointed in equal parts.

'I get how it looks, but I didn't hurt Hugo and neither did Danny. I don't know who did, but it wasn't us. I didn't know anything about the drugs until I phoned Danny and he told me we could help each other out. Which was *after* Hugo was attacked.'

Danny caught my eye.

'Maybe you didn't have anything to do with Hugo's accident, but I wouldn't put it past *him* to have had something to do with it.' Connor looked furious. Together we had dealt with his brother's actions until we'd mostly got him out of our lives, and then I'd brought it all back to our front doorstep. I'd be surprised if Connor ever forgave me for this.

'Well, isn't this just wonderful? We still have at least nine days to go; we have a shit-tonne of illegal drugs on board; and we're sharing a boat with someone who tried to kill one of our friends.' Bella's words were filled with contempt.

Danny leant over the table, his face inches from Bella's. 'I've told you, I did not have anything to do with what happened to Hugo.' His voice was tight, his words dangerous. To her credit, Bella did not flinch, but Connor shoved Danny away.

'Leave her alone.'

Danny turned and smiled a savage smile; a cornered predator

was dangerous, especially a scared one. I needed to do something, I'd seen the looks on my twins' faces a hundred times before, but it had been years since I'd had to stand between them and God only knew how much damage they would inflict now. This boat was not big enough for one of their fights.

'Stop it! Both of you.' I stood between them. 'No matter what I've done, I'm still the skipper of this boat. Connor, you're on mother watch; you and Flick need to finish tidying up. Danny, go up on deck and cool off.'

'I don't–'

'Now!' I stood firm, not having a clue what I would do if he didn't go upstairs. Thankfully I didn't need to find out.

Throughout all of this, Carl had been sitting in a corner on the sofa, just watching. He hadn't said a word. His silence unnerved me.

'Make sure you set an alarm for watch, Erin,' I said and then let myself into my cabin. I needed to be alone for a while.

———

Erin stood in front of the open hatch, yawning and stretching. We were beginning the morning watch and we couldn't yet see the sun heralding the start of another day.

'Are you okay?' Erin asked as she took her place beside me at the helm.

'I'm fine.'

'I'm here for you. You know, if you want to talk?'

'Thanks, but I'd really rather not just now.'

Erin's gaze lingered on me for a few moments before she gazed off towards where the sun was soon to rise.

We spent the next few hours in virtual silence until the hatch slid back just after the sun had fully risen. Erin and I watched to see who would appear. It was Connor.

'You all right?' I asked Connor. He nodded. 'What's up?' There had to be something the matter, I didn't think he'd come up on deck to pass the time of day with me.

'I've been watching the weather.'

'Erin, can you take the wheel, please?' I didn't wait for an answer, I sat down across the table from Connor.

'Tell me.'

'There's a storm gathering. It looks pretty fierce. I'm worried.'

'What? When?'

'Maybe tomorrow afternoon or evening?'

I looked up, but there were no clouds – all that could be seen was a picture-perfect, breathtaking view that wouldn't be out of place in a cruise brochure.

But I knew, from now on, I needed to pay attention to every little thing the weather did. All the subtle changes in the wind, my sense of smell and cloud formations would inform my every decision.

'We're good for now?'

Connor nodded. 'It's too far away to get close to us today.'

'I'll deal with it after watch and we'll make the boat ready then.'

Storms at this time of year were rare, it was the main reason we sailed west in the winter. I was beginning to think this voyage was cursed. Maybe there was something in those old sailors' superstitions after all.

CHAPTER TWENTY-FOUR

THE NORTH ATLANTIC – DAY NINE

Once I'd finished watch, I called a meeting for after breakfast. All I really wanted to do was sleep, but this was too important.

'There's no point in beating about the bush, Connor's spotted a storm that's headed in our direction. A big one. It'll likely be on us by tomorrow evening. We need to spend the day making sure we're as ready as we can be to face it.'

'What are the fucking chances?' Sean groaned.

'There's not a lot I can do about the weather, is there?' I was snapping and I knew it, but complaining about something I had no control over was a surefire way to wind me up.

'We need to make sure everything is stowed, and I mean everything. I don't want stuff crashing around down here. It's going to be dangerous enough as it is without projectiles flying everywhere.'

Everyone looked around, we'd become pretty slack at putting things away; the fine weather making us complacent.

'Let's get some food made ahead of time. We won't be able to use the cooker during the storm, so anything that can be eaten cold is great.'

'We'll do some pasta salad, some sandwiches, that sort of thing.' Nick and Flick were on mother watch. I knew I could rely on Nick: he did not do hungry.

'From tomorrow morning, I want everyone wearing life jackets–' A chorus of groans cut me off. I raised my voice. 'You know the drill. You'll thank me if the boat goes down, or you end up in the water.'

'Do you want me to do mechanical and engine checks?' Sean had his game face on now.

'Please. I'm hoping we can ride out the storm using the engine, but I suspect we may not have enough fuel, which means we'll need to stick to watches. I'll do rigging checks on deck. You won't need to take them until later tonight, but I've got anti-sickness tablets if anyone wants them.' I looked at the serious faces around me. 'It goes without saying, everyone is on standby to help, which means getting as much rest as you can when you can from now on.'

I left Connor with instructions to keep a close eye on the storm and made my way up on deck. I filled Danny and Erin in on the details; Danny said he was happy to cover watch for a while longer, while Erin looked like she was ready to throw up at any second. Danny might not have been the kind of son I would have wished for, but he knew there was nothing for it but to muck in in these circumstances.

The whole crew remained busy for most of the rest of the day. I briefed everyone on emergency procedures, ran through what we'd be doing with the sails, handed out sail ties and lifelines to everyone, and I made sure everyone knew where the EPIRB was. The emergency position-indicating radio beacon was one of the most important pieces of kit in an emergency situation: it could be our only hope of being found if the boat went down and it was important that everyone knew where it was and how to use it.

I could tell we were really starting to freak Erin out when she burst into tears as I showed her the EPIRB. I did not have the patience, but I also needed her to be wholly present.

'I know this all probably seems quite scary, but most of it is just preparedness. It *is* going to get rough and it's not going to be pleasant, and we do most of this to make life as easy as we can during a storm. *If* the worst happens, then we all know what we're doing and what needs to happen. I would far rather we were over-prepared than under-prepared.' I gave Erin what I hoped was a warm smile. 'You are an important member of the crew and I need you to do your bit. I didn't bring you along just for a jolly, you know.'

Erin managed a small smile, which brightened after she blew her nose and wiped her eyes. 'Sorry, I just... well, I wasn't expecting anything like this.'

'To be fair, none of us were. A storm at this time of year is unusual. Perhaps I should have briefed you better, but I honestly didn't think this would ever come up. We'll be fine though; this is where we pull together as a team and support one another. You wait, Sean'll be throwing his guts up before you know it.'

This elicited a small giggle from Erin and I sent her off to double-check her and Bella's cabin.

By late afternoon we were as ready as we could possibly be. It didn't stop me from going over emergency procedures several more times though. I finally stopped when seven people groaned and shouted, 'No more!' at me when I tried to go through them again.

'Mum, please, stop. We've gone over this a million times. We know what we're doing,' Connor said.

I eyeballed him and my stubbornness tried to take over; it wanted to make them listen just one more time. I swallowed it down instead and asked Connor to download some more weather data while I tried the radio to see if there were any other craft nearby. When there was no answer, I decided to use the sat phone to contact Falmouth Coastguard to advise them of our impending predicament.

It could take days for the nearest commercial ship to locate us, but if we gave Falmouth our latest position every three hours or so, at least they'd have somewhere to start looking.

I was grateful I needed to make the call on deck. Although Erin had rallied after my 'motivational' chat earlier, she still looked at me with big eyes, as if her life really were in danger. I was probably being a bit unfair, but her dramatics were not helping anyone and we were, literally, all in the same boat.

Dinner that evening was a sombre affair. We all knew that from sometime tomorrow afternoon, we were in for a torrid twenty-four hours.

'Does anyone else wish the storm would just get here, so we can get it over and done with sooner? All this waiting around is doing my head in.' Flick was the first person to say anything other than please and thank you since we sat down.

'Yes!' Erin was clearly glad to be relieved of the thought. She looked around nervously. 'Has anyone ever sailed through one of these before?'

I smiled and saw some of my crewmates chuckling.

'Of course we have.' Nick answered for us all. 'If you've sailed long-distance and not been caught in some kind of storm, you've had it lucky. What about you though, Bella? This is your first time across the Atlantic, isn't it?'

'Yeah, but I've sailed the Cook Strait in New Zealand; I'm good,' Bella said with a grin on her face.

There were noises of admiration from around the table. The Cook Strait was one of the most notoriously difficult passages of sea to sail. Bella regaled us with her story, which led to others doing the same and we passed a companionable few hours together before watch change for some and bed for everyone else.

The literal calm before the storm.

CHAPTER TWENTY-FIVE

THE NORTH ATLANTIC – DAY TEN

The following morning we woke to a calmer sea than I'd expected. Connor was already at the table eating breakfast and I asked him to download the latest weather reports.

'Already done. It's still coming. Mother Nature is lulling us into a false sense of security. Winds will start picking up just before lunch and we can expect the full force to hit us just after dinner. It'll take a few hours to pass, but with a bit of luck we'll be out of it by morning.'

I nodded and began ticking off my mental to-do list. I'd already been through it yesterday, but giving myself something practical to do stopped me from overthinking and considering all the 'what ifs'. In reality, I was as worried as Erin, but I was a firm believer in not worrying about things I couldn't change. So that morning I chose to concentrate on the things I could have an effect on.

As the winds rose I made sure everyone had their life jackets on and gave strict instructions that from now on, anyone on deck must be attached by a lifeline.

Standing in the cockpit, I used the sat phone to call in our position to Falmouth and advised we were expecting the storm to hit within a few hours. As I ended the call, Jonty waved at me, attracting my attention, and then pointed to the horizon behind him. The skyline was like something from a horror film. The blue sky gave way in a crisp sharp edge to a wall of black and purple. It was coming.

I decided to change all watches to two-hour rotations until after the storm passed. No off watch and no mother watch. There was plenty of food prepared and after an initial flurry of activity where we rigged the storm sails, we would batten down the hatches, but I wanted everyone to be on alert.

That evening we didn't see the sunset. Darkness washed over the seascape as if someone had drawn a curtain. The storm had approached slowly at first and then all at once.

The waves banged against the hull of *Duchess*, sounding like a hammer striking an anvil. The wind and rain howled, adding to the din, which meant the only way we could hear each other was to shout. Even then we had to be inches from an ear to have any chance of being heard.

The yacht was keeled over hard, and moving anywhere was fraught with danger. I could only imagine my face mirrored the fear I saw in the others'. There was no doubt about it, this was one of the most dangerous storms I'd ever sailed and there was nothing we could do but ride it out.

Flick, Danny and Carl succumbed to seasickness and although they made valiant efforts to reach the head, sometimes it was too late. Our crew camaraderie had been fractured irreparably thanks to me and Danny, but when it came to clearing up each others' vomit and looking after each other through a perilous situation, they united admirably. Their actions made me ashamed of mine.

Just before midnight I felt a discernible change in the strength of the storm. We weren't leaning so far over and I only had to raise my voice, rather than shout to be heard. Up on deck, dressed in foul-weather gear, I attached my lifeline. Connor and Carl were on watch and Connor nodded at me, smiling a little.

'It's passing!' he yelled across.

Any non-sailors would have disagreed. It was blacker than hell beyond the edges of the boat. There was no moon and no stars, which meant there was only cloud. The only light came from down below and it didn't reach far beyond the edge of the cockpit. The boat had slowed by a few knots, which meant the wind had slackened, and I wondered if we might not manage a little sleep before morning.

'Who's on next?' I shouted.

'Bella and Sean!'

I nodded and signalled I would speak to them downstairs.

Back down below I gave everyone the good news. 'It's easing off, I think we're through the worst of it. Bella and Sean are up next, but why don't we all try and get some rest? Jonty and Dan, you're on in two.'

There were nods all round, and everyone staggered to their cabins or in the case of Bella and Sean, to watch.

I waited for Connor and Carl to come downstairs and helped them get out of their foul-weather gear and dry off. They both looked utterly exhausted.

'Do you want some food?'

'Not for me, I'm going to get some sleep.' Connor could sleep anywhere and through anything. I let him go, he'd eat when he was hungry.

'Are there any sandwiches left?' Carl asked.

I nodded and gave him one from the fridge. I watched him take a bite and chew, before he swallowed hard.

'Maybe not,' he said and rewrapped the sandwich. 'I'll have it later.'

'Will you be all right?' I did not want him throwing up on his bunk.

'I think so. I'll just sit up a bit.'

I left him to it and made my way into my cabin silently, not bothering to get undressed in case I was needed in a hurry. Flick was already cocooned under her blanket.

I dozed on and off, never fully asleep. I was all too conscious of every bang, every shift *Duchess* made and of the fact I may be called upon at a moment's notice. I wasn't overly concerned though; I was confident Bella and Sean could handle the back end of a storm.

An almighty bang cut through the wind noise and had me sitting up ready for action.

''S the head door.'

'What?'

'The head door. Someone's let go of it and that's what's banged.' Flick's voice was thick with sleep, but she was right and I lay back down.

I must have drifted off, because the next thing I knew, I was being shaken roughly.

'Helen, wake up! It's Bella, she's gone!'

'Gone where?' I asked groggily, in my sleep-befuddled state.

'I think she's gone overboard.'

'What? Shit!' I turned on the light and looked at my watch. Sean was standing in front of me, abject horror splashed across his face. A few seconds later I worked it out.

'Who's manning the helm?'

'Auto-pilot.'

'Get the fuck back up there – now! Flick, get up, get everyone else up and on deck, man overboard!'

I pulled on my foul-weather jacket – my legs could get wet – watching Flick to make sure she had registered my words. The look of understanding and fear confirmed she had.

I raced up the stairs and fastened my lifeline. 'Turn her around. How long since she went in?'

'I don't know, I don't know!'

People were emerging from below deck now. 'Bella's in the water! Use your torches, spread out and keep your eyes peeled. Lifelines ON!'

Terror bubbled up inside me. I'd never lost a crew member before, but I had an awful feeling. It was nearly two in the morning; the storm had lessened but we still had to raise our voices to be heard. I had no idea how long Bella had been in the water, nor where the current was likely to take her. I could only hope her life jacket was enough.

'Was she not strapped on?' I shouted to Sean. Despite the rain, I could still see the tears streaming down his face.

'She was, I'm sure she was.' But Sean's face told me he wasn't really sure of anything right now.

'Have you pressed the man overboard button?'

Sean didn't have to say anything for me to know he'd forgotten. I pressed it and moved to make a mayday call on the VHF on the off-chance there was another vessel in the vicinity.

I ordered someone to turn the engine on, and someone else to get the storm jib down and stowed. We needed to turn around and begin our search in ever-increasing circles.

The key number was fifteen minutes. We had fifteen minutes to get someone out of the water – normally. But normally, we didn't have swells banging off the side of the boat, and normally, we weren't battling a storm, and normally someone saw the person fall in. I knew we had less than fifteen minutes, but crucially, I didn't know when the timer had started.

CHAPTER TWENTY-SIX

THE NORTH ATLANTIC – DAY ELEVEN

Nine of us searched the sea for Bella for hours. We called her name, pausing between each shout, hoping to God we heard something in return. We sailed in circles, widening the diameter each time.

We had to keep going; we could find her at any moment. When I thought about being in the water, with no land for thousands of miles and no certainty of any ships passing, terror swept over me. Even with her life jacket on, Bella had little chance of survival unless we, or another vessel, found her. I tried not to think about it and focused instead on looking for her.

The storm had finally passed and the sun had started to break through and brighten the day. I hoped being able to see further meant we would be more likely to find her, but my hopes were fading fast.

'How long are we going to keep looking for?' Danny was the first to voice a thought I'm sure everyone else was thinking – I knew I was.

'For as long as it takes,' Sean snapped.

'Don't be ridiculous. We might never find her,' Carl replied.

Sean growled and took a step towards him.

'Stop it! Just stop it!' Flick screamed at them through tears.

I looked around at my crew; every single one of them was ready to drop from sheer exhaustion. I called them together in the cockpit.

'We've been searching for hours and not seen or heard anything. There has been nothing from any other ships on the VHF either. I know Falmouth have diverted them to help with the search, but there's been no word. I don't know what to do for the best. As much as I hate to say it, Danny's right, we can't search forever.'

Flick sobbed, her face now buried in her hands. Erin's face was pale, but I could see her eyes still searching the sea behind me. The boys were stoney-faced, all looking to the sea as they listened to my words. Only Danny made eye contact.

'We can't just leave her here,' Connor said, glancing at me.

'Of course we can't. We'll keep searching.' Jonty glared at me, daring me to contradict him.

I nodded and looked at my watch. 'We'll keep searching for another few hours, but if we don't find her, we need to make a difficult decision.' I took in the faces of my crew. 'We're all knackered, I'm splitting us into two groups. The first needs to go and get some sleep, while the rest of us search. We'll switch in an hour.'

Six hours later there was still no sign of Bella. For the second time that day, I called my crew to the cockpit. I noticed each of them was still scanning the water as I spoke.

'We've been searching for over fifteen hours. As much as it pains me to say it, I don't think we're going to find her.' I paused, giving everyone the chance to contradict me if they wanted to. No one did. 'I think we have to… um… I think we have to accept she's gone and carry on to St Lucia.' Even as I said the words, tears pricked at my eyes. I swallowed hard and stared at the sky trying desperately to blink them away.

Around me I could hear sniffing and throats being cleared. Erin and Flick were crying, and Connor was trying hard not to. Even Danny, a man I considered heartless, looked devastated.

'If anyone has anything they'd like to suggest, or say, now is the time.' No one would be able to say I hadn't considered all options.

'I think we should keep looking. The only reason you want to stop is so you don't lose money.' Sean may as well have slapped me.

There was a collective intake of breath, my own included. It was no secret I had a soft spot for Sean, and we'd grown close on the journey so far, but in that moment I hated him.

'Don't be a prick, Sean.' Jonty came to my rescue.

'Thank you.'

'Don't think this means we're okay now. I'm still pissed off, but I happen to think you're right on this one.' Jonty put me firmly in my place.

'Fine.' There was no point in dwelling on it. 'Anyone else?'

There were head shakes all around. As if no one else wanted to say we were giving up out loud. As if it somehow absolved them of having to make, or agree with a horrific decision.

After giving everyone enough time to speak up, I stood to fetch the sat phone. I needed to inform Falmouth of our thoughts and get their permission to leave the area.

'What I want to know is, what happened? How did she fall in without anyone seeing? And why wasn't she tied on?' Jonty sounded exhausted, but there was an edge to his voice.

Despite losing Bella only a few short hours ago, I knew this would remain with us for the rest of our lives. I also knew if I thought about it for too long, it would render me immobile, both physically and psychologically. Even more so now, I felt a responsibility to make sure each and every person on board this boat made it to St Lucia in one piece. Only then could I stand down.

'I think we'd all like to know the answer to that, but no one knows, do they?' Nick said. I could always rely on him to be the voice of reason.

'Well, someone knows something. Don't they, Sean?' Jonty said, pointedly.

Sean glanced up at the sound of his name; he'd been staring at his feet. 'I...' His face paled as he took in the looks from his crewmates.

My heart went out to him and I could believe the level of guilt consuming him at the moment, but at the same time, we deserved some answers. I'd been concentrating on trying to find Bella, but now was ready for an explanation.

'Why don't you tell us what happened?' I tried to be gentle.

Sean swallowed hard and closed his eyes. We all watched him expectantly, trying to be patient and allow him time to gather his thoughts.

When he opened his eyes again, there was a hardness to them and he stared at the horizon. 'I didn't feel well. I had a pain in my stomach and I needed to get to the head – quickly.' Sean's face coloured at the admission. 'I shouted to Bella, told her where I was going and said to make sure she was tied on. I didn't stop to check. I said it, not because I thought I needed to, but because that's just what you say, right?' He looked around for confirmation; I took pity on him and nodded.

'I think I was in there for maybe ten minutes. I tried to hurry, but when you've got diarrhoea there's not a lot you can do. I realised after it was too late I should've asked someone to cover for me...' Sean was right, he should've but there was little point in reinforcing the point now. 'When I made it back on deck, there was no one at the wheel. I took control and looked around, but I couldn't see her anywhere. I set cruise control and woke Helen. The rest you know.'

I couldn't help but feel sorry for Sean and angry with him all at the same time. He *should* have been fine to leave the deck for ten minutes, but good practice was good practice for a *reason* and he knew that. He had enough experience to understand why we did what we did. It was supposed to become like breathing – natural, a habit you couldn't help but continue. Thinking about it, it could've happened to anyone, but it didn't, it happened to Sean and now he was going to have to live with the guilt. Live with the 'what if' questions he would surely have, we would *all* surely have, forever.

It was time to make the difficult call. I didn't really have an option; we couldn't sail around in circles in the middle of the Atlantic indefinitely. I sat in the cockpit staring out to sea for a full ten minutes. I allowed my mind to relax, flex and wander. When I didn't come up with another, realistic solution or suggestion in that time I knew what I had to do. And it had to be me. I couldn't ask anyone else to take on the level of responsibility. Even though I hadn't acted like a skipper in Gran Canaria, I could be one now and alleviate any potential guilt my crew might end up feeling.

'I've made my decision.' I raised my voice to make sure I had their attention, even if they weren't looking at me. 'We're going to continue to St Lucia – now. We've searched for over fifteen,' I looked at my watch, 'sixteen hours now, I think we have to accept she's gone.'

Connor stood and moved to stand beside Carl at the helm. Neither of them were looking at me, but that was only unusual for Connor.

'You just want to make sure you get your money,' Sean said contemptuously. I didn't blame him for being angry. It didn't matter what I said about the money, he wasn't going to believe me, but I was going to try.

'That's irrelevant. My decision would still be the same.'

'I don't believe you.'

I sighed. I'd failed them miserably and didn't deserve their trust, so I didn't ask for it.

'I think we'll move to six-hour rotating watches. It doesn't matter who's with who–'

'Have you seen this?' Connor interrupted me.

I looked over to where he was standing, my hands still mid-gesticulation. 'What is it?'

Connor was looking at something down by his feet near the side of the boat. He crouched down, fiddling with something on the deck. When he stood up he was holding what looked like a scrap of material in his hand. He held it high and let it dangle from his fingers.

It was a lifeline. Or more accurately, it was half a lifeline, the edge might as well have been razor sharp.

It had been cut. Sliced through – deliberately.

CHAPTER TWENTY-SEVEN

C ut. *It's been cut.*

It was all I could think. There were no frayed edges, it was a clean slice. There couldn't have been frayed edges anyway. We checked and double-checked all the equipment before we left Scotland, and then again before we left Gran Canaria. I was fastidious about this sort of thing. Even a lifeline that was a tiny bit frayed on the edges would not have been allowed on one of my boats, let alone a lifeline that was so badly damaged it could have snapped. Except lifelines can't snap – that's the whole point of them. They're made of a blend of materials that ensure they are strong enough to withstand the heaviest of pulls.

Even if a frayed lifeline had somehow got on board, that wasn't what had happened here. The lifeline Connor was holding up for us all to see had a crisp, sharp edge. Only a knife, and a very sharp one at that, could have made that edge. I'm not sure even scissors would have been enough to get through the dense webbing.

Even in the few seconds after Connor showed us what he had found, after the truth had come crashing down around me, I realised this changed everything. Yet it changed nothing. We would still need to continue towards the Caribbean; a cut lifeline didn't increase our chances of finding Bella in the water. What it did mean though, was that someone had cut her lifeline. I shuddered. It meant that *someone* was on my boat.

I looked around me, wondering if anyone had come to the same startling conclusion I had. Their pale faces and wide eyes told me they had. Connor and Carl exchanged a look and I wondered... No, surely not?

'It's been cut.' Erin's whisper was barely audible, but yet we all heard it. Perhaps because we'd all been thinking it.

'How can you possibly know that?' Flick snapped.

'I-I-'

'Flick, stop it. It's quite obvious it's been cut; you don't need to be an experienced sailor to tell that.' Nick's words were firm yet sympathetic as he gestured towards where Connor stood, the half lifeline still in his hand.

'Aw, isn't that sweet. Defending your girlfriend.' I glared at Danny, now was not the time.

'She's not my-' Nick started to rise to the bait and then checked himself. 'I'd do the same for any of you.'

I turned to Nick. Had I missed something? *Were* he and Erin a couple? Did I mind? Nick was one of my closest friends; did it bother me that they might have been seeing each other and not told me? But they'd only met each other when we boarded *Duchess*. Surely I would know? I'd have seen something?

Nick's cheeks coloured slightly, and I realised that while they might not be a couple, there was a bit of truth in what Danny had said. *Well done for paying attention to your crew, Helen!*

'We should be having watches of three.' Jonty did that thing where he voiced his opinion as fact.

'Why?' Flick had spotted it too, and was aiming her fear and anger at the easiest target – her ex-husband.

'Because it would be safer.' Erin was staring at the table in front of her, speaking to no one in particular.

Flick stared at her. Did she not understand? Or was she too stunned to speak?

'If we have watches of two, then someone could easily push their watch partner overboard. With watches of three there would be a witness so it's less likely to happen.' Trust Carl to be so blunt. 'Unless of course two people are working together to bump us all off.' Carl grinned, but now was not the time for gallows humour and his poorly timed 'joke' fell flat.

'Surely no one would–'

'Someone cut Bella's lifeline! For fuck sake, Erin! How can you be so naive, you write books for a living.' Jonty slammed his hand down on the table, making us all jump. 'I'm sorry, but we all have to get used to the idea that one of us made that cut, and therefore it's likely whoever did that also pushed Bella overboard. It wasn't an accident.' He dropped the volume now he had our attention.

We were all looking at one another and I wondered if they were doing the same as me. Were they trying to read their crewmates? Trying to look into their eyes and see if they were a killer? What did a killer even look like? Most pictures of killers I'd seen had a kind of haunting in their eyes; they looked as if there was no life there. The people around me looked exhausted and scared, not evil.

Jonty was right though, watches of three made more sense given the circumstances.

'We'll do six-hour watches of three, rotation starts at 6am. You'll have twelve hours off in between.' People were nodding in agreement around me. 'At least then if someone needs to go to the toilet during the night, no one will be left on deck alone.'

Sean flinched as if he'd been physically struck. It was harsh, but I was angry. He might not have been responsible for Bella ending up in the water, but he should never have left her on her own either. He had to bear some of the responsibility, I didn't have the strength to take it all on myself.

I split everyone into their new watches and nominated myself to make us something to eat. I doubted anyone was hungry, but I needed to keep myself busy and the crew needed to keep their strength up.

I was grateful no one seemed to be in the mood for conversation, not with me or each other. I wanted to be alone with my thoughts, and on a yacht in the middle of nowhere, quiet was about as close as you got to being alone.

So far on this voyage one of my crew had been beaten to within an inch of his life; I'd allowed my son to smuggle drugs on board; another crew member had suffered a horrific anaphylactic shock and then a few days later, apparently, been pushed overboard. They say in life you make your own luck. They're usually talking about good luck, but I was beginning to wonder if that's true of bad luck too.

I snorted.

'Penny for them?' Nick was watching me from the chart table.

I wondered whether to tell him or not and then, 'I was just thinking about how much bad luck one person could take before they came to the conclusion the world was out to get them.'

'No, she didn't have much luck while she was on board, did she?'

'Who?' It took me too long to realise he meant Bella.

'Bella. Who were you talking about?'

I concentrated on slicing the cheese in front of me. When I looked up, Nick was still staring at me, his eyes wide. 'Please tell me you weren't talking about yourself?'

I didn't reply, the flush in my cheeks was enough for him though.

'Jesus Christ, Helen. This is too much even for you. *You* got yourself into this mess, Bella never did anything to deserve it.

And neither did Hugo for that matter. Get a grip.' Nick stood abruptly just as the hatch opened above his head.

He stepped out of the way and Jonty tumbled down the steps, closely followed by Sean.

'I've worked out who it was.'

CHAPTER TWENTY-EIGHT

Nick moved backwards to get out of Jonty and Sean's way. The chart-table seat banging him in the back of the legs caused him to sit down heavily.

I braced myself and took a step forward, alert. Alert for what, I didn't know, but Jonty's words had created an urgency my body automatically responded to.

'I'm pretty sure I know who did it,' he said, out of breath as if he'd run much further than the dozen or so paces it took to get down below.

'He's talking shite.' Sean's face was red and his eyes wide.

'What are you talking about, Jonty?' I asked.

'It all makes sense, doesn't it? There's only one person who could have pushed Bella overboard *and* got away with it.' Jonty's focus was on me.

'It could've been anyone. I was in the head for ages.' Sean was no longer scared; I'm sure if he'd been an animal he would have been baring his teeth by now.

'So you say.'

By now, Erin and Flick had joined us. Connor, Danny and

Carl were on watch; I counted everyone off in my head out of habit, caught for a second when I realised I was a person short.

We were all standing, apart from Nick, who was now sitting at the chart table properly, out of the way. It was crowded and the atmosphere had begun to feel claustrophobic, even for me and I was used to tiny spaces.

Jonty and Sean were arguing. If you could call it that, since they weren't actually listening to each other, just talking louder and louder expecting the other to back down.

It was too much.

'Shut up.' They didn't hear me. 'SHUT UP!'

Everyone stopped and turned to me. Jonty opened his mouth and I held up my hand.

'Nope. Stop. Everybody sit down.'

'I–'

'Jonty, sit the fuck down!' Everyone else was shuffling around to take a seat, Jonty just stared. I glared back at him; I was not in the mood for taking any shit.

When he eventually took his seat, my pointed finger swung back and forth, jabbing between Jonty and Sean as I spoke. 'Now, does one of you two want to tell me what the fuck is going on?'

'Jonty thinks it was me who cut Bella's lifeline and pushed her overboard.' Sean spoke with a false bravado.

'Hang on, no one's actually said anyone pushed Bella overboard.' I was clutching at straws, but it made me feel a tiny bit better for a second.

'Oh, come on, Helen! Her lifeline was *cut*. Who's going to do that and just leave it? What possible reason could there be?'

I conceded Jonty's point with a slight nod and moved on. 'Fine, but what makes you think it was Sean?'

'He was the only person up there with her, wasn't he? I mean, he said he had the shits and was in the head for ten minutes, but we've only got his word for that.'

'Okay, assuming you're right,' I held up my hand to silence Sean's impending outburst, 'I have one question. Why? Why would Sean want to... kill Bella?' The words felt alien in my mouth. Even saying them out loud didn't make it feel real. 'Because that's what we're talking about here, isn't it? You push someone overboard in the middle of the night out here and you're not expecting to fish them out the water, are you?'

'Exactly, why on earth would I want to get rid of Bella?' Sean was clinging on to the life raft I'd thrown him.

'I don't know, do I?'

'Exactly! I've no reason to want her dead. You can't just accuse me of something because it fits your version of events.'

'Oh, but you want us to accept your version of events? Just because you say so?'

'There was someone in the head.' Flick spoke quickly, the words pouring out of her mouth like water.

Everyone paused.

'Shit, you're right.' I'd forgotten about the banging head door.

'How do you know?' Jonty sneered.

'We heard the door bang just before we went to sleep. You know, like it does when you don't keep hold of it properly and the boat tilts and it slips out of your hand. Helen and I both heard it.'

'That could've been anyone. And as for why, you might have had some sort of lovers' tiff before, when you met on that website.' Jonty wasn't letting this go.

'Plenty of Fish?' Sean asked, a little surprised.

'That's the one!' Jonty sounded like someone had just given him the winning answer to a pub quiz, instead of someone in the midst of accusing murder.

'But we only chatted online, we never actually met in person. Even Bella told you that.'

'But you did say she was beginning to sound like a bit of a bunny boiler.'

Sean's face coloured. 'As if that's a reason to kill someone.'

'People have killed for less,' Nick murmured. I shot him a look. 'Sorry, shouldn't have said that.'

'Maybe it was you, Jonty.' I'd almost forgotten Erin was there.

'What exactly are you implying?' Flick had put on her best yachty accent, but it didn't hide the fear in her eyes.

'I'm just making a suggestion. Jonty seems to think Sean has a valid reason for wanting Bella gone, but Jonty's reason is stronger. Bella ruined your marriage; she also cost you a lot of money in the divorce I'll wager, Jonty.'

Jonty spluttered and turned red as he tried to form the words to reply to Erin.

'Don't be ridiculous,' Flick said contemptuously. 'Jonty is a lot of things, but he wouldn't murder someone. True, he was angry with Bella, but killing her achieves nothing.'

Sean saw an opportunity to join in with the finger-pointing. 'You would defend him. Or, maybe it was you. Maybe you were the angry one and you saw the opportunity present itself? You said yourself you heard someone going into the head.'

'Oh, fuck off, Sean!' Flick said, and Jonty growled.

This whole... meeting, if you could call it that, was about to descend into an argument filled with vitriol. I couldn't allow the situation to get any more out of control than it already was. 'Enough! Blaming each other isn't going to get us anywhere. And for what it's worth, Flick was in our bunk, with me, the entire time. As you well know, Sean, she was there when you woke me up.'

Nobody said anything.

'True,' Sean said eventually, conceding the point like a petulant child.

'I get we're all scared, angry, upset and a whole host of other emotions, but accusing each other isn't going to help. We have another week or so of sailing to go and we need to stick together to make sure we get there in one piece. After that, the police can take over,' I said.

'And everyone seems to be forgetting the little matter of the drugs handover.'

'Why are you bringing that up now?'

Yeah, thanks for that, Erin.

CHAPTER TWENTY-NINE

THE NORTH ATLANTIC – DAY FOURTEEN

The next couple of days passed as peacefully as they could. At least everyone had stopped accusing one another, for the moment, but the air of suspicion was never far away. Someone on board had cut Bella's lifeline, and because we could see no other answer, this meant they had also pushed her into the Atlantic and left her for dead. Only one person knew who that was, and they weren't saying anything. Tensions were high and everyone's actions were scrutinised by amateur detectives looking for clues.

I knew it wasn't me, and if you forced me to guess who I thought it might be, I couldn't. I couldn't imagine a single person on board *Duchess* being callous enough to throw someone overboard in the middle of a never-ending ocean. Yes, Danny could be a nasty piece of work and I wouldn't put a bit of intimidation, or assault and battery past him, but I could not conceive of a world where one of my sons would deliberately kill someone, particularly in such a cold-hearted manner. Bella had been the one to voice the idea of disposing of the drugs, but I was sure we all ended up on the same page on that one.

Since losing Bella, I'd found it difficult to sleep for more than a couple of hours at a time. Thinking of her floating around, with no real hope of survival or being found, kept my mind busy on a constant loop. I'd spent a lot of time talking to Erin about how important rest was, but now I found myself up and drinking coffee before she was awake most mornings.

Erin had retreated into herself and when she wasn't on watch, she was either scribbling in her notebook or tapping away on her computer. While I was glad our plan to inspire her had worked, I couldn't help but find it insensitive that something good was happening for her, in amongst what I could easily name the worst voyage of my life.

The atmosphere on board was tense and morose, and each day seemed as long as two. I'd taken to counting down the miles to St Lucia in an effort to keep everyone positive. Nobody said anything though, so I don't think it worked. Having said that, there were some moments when I announced another mile marker where I felt more positive, so I kept going on the off-chance someone else felt the same as I did.

As we grew closer to the Caribbean, the weather evened out, and, other than the odd, brief squall, we had wall-to-wall sunshine. We broke out our sunglasses and caps, and slathered ourselves in sunscreen.

It was on day fourteen, three days after Bella disappeared and with, hopefully, only five or six days to go, that I decided to try the sat phone again. I carried it to the front of the boat and sat down on the deck by myself. It was one of the few places on board, apart from the head, where you were likely to be by yourself. I was craving solitude.

While I waited for the sat phone to connect, my thoughts wandered to Danny and the drugs. As far as I knew, some kind of motorised yacht would be coming out to meet us a day or two before we landed in St Lucia. According to Danny, they would 'be in contact'. I had no idea how since I couldn't imagine them using the VHF and they didn't have the sat phone number. I tried to tell myself it wasn't my problem, but I knew if they didn't pick up their drugs before we landed, it would very much be my problem.

After a few minutes the sat phone pinged indicating, not only did we have a connection, but there was a voicemail as well. I quickly dialled in and listened to the message. It was from the police in Gran Canaria. Hugo had woken up and they were asking me to call as soon as possible.

I returned the call and waited what seemed like an age for the connection to be made. I imagined a beam of green light shooting up into the sky from my phone, and then bouncing around various satellites surrounded by stars, before finally charging back down to earth and landing in Gran Canaria.

Someone eventually answered, but it wasn't the person I needed to speak to. I was left waiting again while the correct person was found.

'Hello, is this Helen Johnstone, captain of the yacht, *Duchess?*' I recognised the voice of the detective who had driven Sean and me to the hospital.

'Yes, that's right. How's Hugo? Is he awake?'

'The doctors woke Hugo up from his coma two days ago. Sadly, he has no memory of that night. Not yet anyway. The doctors say it's possible that it will come back, but also that it may never come back.'

Well that was as clear as mud, wasn't it? I found myself unusually emotional and took a moment to compose myself.

'Is he okay otherwise? Is he going to make a full recovery?' I swallowed down the emotion, grateful to the wind for drying my tears, and tried to get as much information as I could to relay to the crew.

'He has a lot of bruising and there is still some swelling on his head, but the doctors are confident he will make a full recovery, physically at least.'

'That's something.' Except I knew that mental scars and recovery were often ten times worse than physical ones.

'Señora Johnstone, I was wondering if there was anything else you could tell me?'

'Tell you? We discussed everything I know while I was in Gran Canaria.'

'Yes, but I wondered if you might have remembered anything differently? Or if, perhaps one of your crew said anything? You managed to fill the space on your boat quickly, no?'

'Er, yes. My other son was available at short notice.' Where was he going with this?

'I see. I wonder why he wasn't on the original list of crew members? Since, as you say, he is your son and therefore you must know him extremely well.'

Now that was a bloody good point, but there was no way I could tell him the truth. Being honest would raise all sorts of red flags. Instead, I said, 'The rest of the crew were paying and I needed the income.'

'I see.'

'Was there anything else?' I just wanted to get off the phone.

'No, that is all for now.'

'Okay, would you call back if Hugo remembers anything? I know his crewmates are all eager to hear news.'

'Of course. *Adiós*, Señora Johnstone.'

I said my goodbye and then ended the call with a sigh of relief. I wasn't out of the woods yet, but at least I had some breathing space.

I took a moment to gather myself and then made my way back to the cockpit, a smile on my face. Surely now, upon hearing that Hugo was awake and would recover at least physically, everyone would raise their spirits and the last few days on board, in the sunshine, would be harmonious if nothing else.

CHAPTER THIRTY

Connor was manning the helm, while Danny and Carl sat in the cockpit chatting. I wondered if either of them ever did their bit, but I was picking my fights and this one didn't seem like it was worth pursuing. This boat was rocking enough as it was, I wasn't about to add to it unless I absolutely had to.

'Good news,' I announced, waving, once I was within hearing distance. 'Hugo's woken up!'

'Is that so?' replied Danny.

At the very least I had expected some kind of positive reaction, but Danny and Carl were indifferent.

'Cool,' was Carl's only response.

I turned to Connor; he did not let me down. 'That's great news! Does he remember anything?'

I often thought of Danny and Connor as the characters from the film *Twins*, with Danny DeVito and Arnold Schwarzenegger. Except, with my two, one had all the anger and aggression, and the other had all the calm and serenity.

'Not so far. The doctors don't know if his memory will ever fully recover, but they've also said it could come back in a few days. No one knows for sure.'

'Shame. Still, at least he's awake, and he's going to be all right?'

'The policeman I spoke to said the doctors believe he'll make a full physical recovery.'

Connor screwed his face up, perhaps having come to the same conclusion as I had about mental scars being more difficult to heal.

'I'm going down to tell the others.'

Down in the saloon, Erin was sitting at the table, her head down and earphones in, tapping ferociously at her laptop. I rolled my eyes, but I wasn't surprised, she spent almost every moment she wasn't on watch in front of her screen.

Nick was sitting at the other end of the table, a coffee in front of him and a book in his hand. It was Connor's copy of *Jamaica Inn;* it must have been doing the rounds. Jonty was in the kitchen buttering some bread, but Sean and Flick were missing.

'Where are Sean and Flick? Are they sleeping?'

'They've just gone in, not two minutes before you came down,' Jonty answered.

I knocked on Flick's door first and asked her to come and sit in the saloon for a few minutes, before doing the same with Sean.

While I waited for everyone to stop fidgeting, I realised how odd it was that no one had asked why I'd called them all together. Normally there were at least one or two people who couldn't wait and started throwing out questions. Glancing around, I could see that only Flick and Jonty were looking at me, everyone else was staring at something, or nothing, in front of them. Apart from Erin, of course, who still had her eyes on her screen.

'Can you...' I gestured towards Erin and Flick gave her a nudge. Erin looked up and, realising we were waiting for her, she pulled out her earphones and closed her laptop.

'Sorry.'

'No worries.' I plastered the smile back on my face. I *was* pleased Hugo was awake and would be okay, but there were so many other things going on that meant smiling did not come easily. 'I have some good news. I've just been speaking to the police in Gran Canaria and Hugo is awake.'

'Oh, that's wonderful news.' Flick was the first to speak, and the others vocalised their agreement.

'Does he remember who did it?' When Erin asked her question, the group fell silent as if they'd had to be reminded of the terrible thing that caused Hugo to be in hospital in the first place.

'No. Not yet anyway. Apparently the doctors don't know if or when he might remember. On the positive side, he will make a full physical recovery.'

The smiles returned.

We continued chatting for a little while and it almost seemed like things were back to normal. We felt like the crew we had been when we set sail for Gran Canaria, before Hugo's accident, before the drugs, Bella's allergic reaction and... the rest.

Soon, Flick and Sean started yawning and decided to head back to their bunks for some rest, as they had intended before I roused them to make my announcement. Jonty and Nick seemed in a somewhat buoyant mood and decided they were going to do some fishing off the back of the yacht.

I wasn't sure what I wanted to do. We were due on watch in a few hours, and I probably needed to get some rest since we were on until midnight, but I didn't feel tired. I thought about finding a book to read and relaxing for a few hours – completely unheard of for me, but why not? I knew Erin would continue on her laptop with her earphones in and I would have as much peace as I desired for a little while.

I browsed the ten or so paperbacks stored in one of the lockers – there had been an agreement to put them in one place, so others could read them too – and after a short deliberation selected *In The Blink of An Eye* by Jo Callaghan – I remembered Flick saying she'd enjoyed it. After filling my water bottle, I settled down on the sofa and began to read.

'Helen, I need to talk to you.' I was approximately five pages in when Erin stopped typing and removed her headphones, interrupting me.

As she spoke I realised she was vocalising thoughts I had been trying desperately to ignore.

CHAPTER THIRTY-ONE

'But seriously, if you think about it, it makes perfect sense.' Erin was not about to let this go.

I sat back and the leather squeaked in protest. I needed a minute to think, but she kept talking.

'It answers all the questions we've been asking.' She sounded almost ecstatic.

But does it?

It wasn't as if hearing Erin say it out loud was the first time it had occurred to me, but I was trying to get my head around it now someone else appeared to agree with me, albeit without them realising. And I might be able to if she'd just allow her words to sink in and let me process them.

'Hang on,' I said, my hand held up as if to physically stop her words. 'Just... hang on.' I closed my eyes and tried to apply logic. I couldn't see her, but I was acutely aware of Erin's eyes on me in anticipation of an answer.

Eventually I opened my eyes and sat forward in my seat. The index finger of my right hand tapped slowly on the table, emphasising my words. 'So... you're saying, that everything that's happened is because of Danny?'

'Yes! That's exactly what I'm saying.'

'You think Danny attacked Hugo, because he "knew" I would call him and ask him to help me? And this was all part of his plan to smuggle the drugs to the Caribbean?' I was whispering now; sound travelled on a boat and even with the noise of the wind, I needed to be sure no one could overhear us.

'It might not have been Danny who attacked Hugo; it could have been one of his mates, Carl or someone, but the point is, he orchestrated it.'

I wasn't convinced Danny would even know what the word "orchestrated" meant, but Erin had a point – maybe.

'Danny might just have seen an opportunity and capitalised on it,' I pointed out.

Erin was thoughtful. 'Yeah, you could be right, but it's a helluva coincidence, don't you think?'

She was right on that. It just all seemed a little *too* neat. I moved on. 'Do you really think he had something to do with Bella as well?'

Erin nodded furiously, she'd obviously put a lot of thought into her theory. 'I also think Bella's allergic reaction was the first time he tried.'

'Woah!' It hadn't even crossed my mind the milk in Bella's coffee *hadn't* been a terrible accident and a thoughtless mistake on Sean's part.

Sean again? I wasn't going to put him in Erin's crosshairs by saying his name out loud though.

'What are the chances of Bella having an allergic reaction and her EpiPen going missing – *at the same time*? Everyone had been so careful to make sure they didn't accidentally give her anything with cow's milk in it.'

'But Danny helped to save her with his own EpiPen.'

'True, but he was hardly going to refuse to let you use it once you'd asked for it, was he?'

'But why bother with… all that in the first place then?'

Erin shrugged. 'I don't have all the answers, but there's a lot of evidence that points to Danny.'

Evidence… was there?

'Okay, assuming that's all true. And Danny really is responsible for… everything,' I waved my arms around vaguely, 'it doesn't answer the question of *why*. Why would Danny want Bella out of the picture?'

'I would have thought that was the most obvious bit.'

I gave Erin a look which hopefully conveyed the message, *clearly not.*

Erin rolled her eyes. 'When Connor found the drugs and there was that argument down here, Bella wanted to throw them overboard to get rid of them. She was pretty vocal about it.'

'She was, but she knew, the same as everyone else did, why that couldn't happen. We talked it through; she'd accepted it, the same as we all had. Although…' I stumbled over the thought, aware of Erin looking at me expectantly. 'Maybe Danny thought she might go to the police once we arrived on dry land?'

'Exactly.' Erin looked excited to have me on her wavelength. Excited was not an emotion I would normally associate with this kind of conversation.

'Having said that,' I was aware I was thinking aloud, 'I never heard her say as much. Did you?'

'No, I can't say that I did. But I did overhear them arguing.'

'What? Way to bury the lede, Erin. What were they arguing about?'

'Well, I think Danny found Bella in the skipper's cabin.'

'You think?'

'Yeah–'

'And how did you overhear them? There's basically nowhere to hide on this boat.'

'I was in the head, they were talking right outside. Kinda like, shouty whispers. Danny was clearly pissed off with her, but Bella was fighting her corner.'

What I couldn't understand was, with everything that had gone on while we were on board, why was I only hearing about this now? I put the question to Erin with a follow-up. 'Is it because he's my son?'

Erin looked a little taken aback. 'No, nothing like that. I hadn't planned to say anything at all. I didn't want to be in Danny's sights, not if he was capable of throwing someone off a boat into the middle of the Atlantic.'

I winced. Shocked she'd made it sound so pedestrian, as if Danny attached no value to a human life, and I was still sure that wasn't the case.

'So why now?'

'Because it's been driving me mad. I can't stop thinking about it and the more it whirls round in my head, the more I knew I had to tell someone. And since you're the skipper – and his mother – well, you drew the short straw.'

I rubbed the top of my nose with two fingers. 'So what was the argument about?' I asked, somehow simultaneously incredulous *and* resigned to the fact that I needed to take this seriously.

'Danny was telling Bella to stay out of his business, and Bella was saying that it was everyone's business now. That Danny had made it our business as soon as he stowed the drugs on board and we left Gran Canaria. Danny said what he always says, not to worry about it and he would deal with it, blah, blah, blah. Bella pointed out that was all very well in theory, but not quite so easy in practice when there was the very real possibility that we could all be arrested in a foreign country for drug smuggling. And fifteen years in a St Lucian prison was very likely to be completely different to fifteen years in a UK prison.'

'For fuck sake. I wish you'd told me all this earlier. Even if you'd just told me about the argument.'

'Why? What could you have done?'

'I could've had a word with Danny for a start.'

'Pfft. He's never listened to you before. Why would he start now?' Erin had a point, but not one I was willing to concede easily.

'You still should've told me.'

'Well, I've told you now. So what are you going to do about it?'

I pondered her question for a minute. It was a good one and I didn't have a ready answer. Eventually, I said, 'Nothing. If Danny really did kill Bella for speaking up – and I'm still not totally convinced he did – then he's not going to think twice about doing it again, is he? We'll be on dry land in a few days, minus the drugs, and then I'll decide what to do.'

Erin shrugged. 'It's your call, but I'll be watching my back from now on.' She put her headphones back in – this conversation was over.

She was right, it was my call, and I could only hope I was making the right one. I picked up my book, determined to carry on reading and enjoy what little relaxation time I had left.

Two pages later it came to me.

'The skipper's cabin!'

CHAPTER THIRTY-TWO

O f course! Why hadn't I thought of it before?

Erin was already back wrapped up in her laptop and hadn't noticed my excitement. I stood and shook her arm. She pulled out her headphones, frowning at me.

'We need to check the skipper's cabin.' I was already halfway up the stairs.

'What for?' Erin asked, following me.

I stopped and turned slightly, leaning down to talk to her. 'What if Danny didn't push Bella overboard? What if he just put her in the skipper's cabin? He might've just wanted to keep her quiet for a bit.'

'That makes no sense. For a start, what if someone went in there and for another thing, that doesn't stop her telling the police about the drugs when we get there.'

'Maybe he thinks it'll be enough to scare her. Plus, there's no reason for anyone to go down there anymore. We're so close to the end, all our supplies are in the kitchen. Plus, everyone knows that's where the drugs are, so everyone's been avoiding it. You know what Danny's been like. Have you been anywhere near it?'

'No...'

'Exactly! Are you coming?' I turned to carry on.

'Hang on a minute,' Erin said, tugging on the bottom of my jacket.

I turned and sat on a step. 'What?'

'Let's just think about this for a second.'

I sighed. 'Fine… what is it you want me to think about?'

'Two things actually. First of all, wouldn't we have heard Bella calling for help? And secondly, going up the front during a storm is dangerous, this was one of the first things you taught me. Surely, trying to drag an uncooperative person up there is going to be even more dangerous. I can't imagine Bella would have gone willingly.'

'You might be right about all of that, but do you know what? I'm checking anyway, because I don't want to know how it feels if we get to St Lucia and find out Bella has been stuck in that hellhole of a cabin for a week.' I turned and continued up the last couple of stairs, sliding back the hatch. I stopped and turned to face Erin. 'And also, why *wouldn't* I? It's the easiest thing in the world to do and I really don't understand why you're putting obstacles in my way.'

Danny and Carl were still sitting in the cockpit and it looked like they hadn't moved. I ignored them, hoping I could make it to the skipper's cabin skylight before they wondered what I was up to. I didn't even stop to check if Erin was following me.

I heard Danny's shout as I pulled up the hatch. 'Hey! What are you doing?'

I turned and saw him rushing towards me, charging past Erin. I ignored him, pulled up the hatch and peered inside. Despite the brightness of the day, and how small the cabin was, there were shadows cast in the corners and I couldn't see inside properly. I climbed down and looked around.

Nothing. Bella wasn't here and I was surprised to find tears filling my eyes. I'd almost managed to convince myself Bella was down here and everything would be all right in the end. I'd allowed myself to believe she was alive and Danny was just trying to teach her a lesson. Now though, I knew, I just *knew* Bella was gone. There was no miracle that meant a passing ship had spotted her low in the sea and rescued her. Bella had either died from drowning, or exposure, and I didn't know which was worse. Fleetingly, and guiltily, I hoped she was dead before she even went in the water – it seemed more humane somehow.

A shadow loomed over me. 'What are you doing in here?' Danny did nothing to hide the aggression in his voice.

I looked up, and between the sun and the tears in my eyes I couldn't make out his features and that somehow stripped him of his ferocity. I stood up and despite him being above me, I swelled with power.

'I was looking for Bella.'

'Bella? But why would you–'

'I thought she might be down here, being kept prisoner...' Even as I said it, I heard how ridiculous it sounded in the harsh light of day and the power slid from me into a puddle on the floor.

'You thought *I'd* attacked Bella and what? *Kidnapped* her?' My accusation had stripped the anger from him and his aggression had been replaced with hurt.

To cover my embarrassment, and give me time to think of a response, I climbed out of the cabin and shut the hatch behind me.

Attack, as the saying goes, is the best form of defence.

'It's not like it's outwith the realms of possibility, is it?' I replied, scornfully.

'Because I'm a drug dealer I must be a violent bastard as well?'

'You're telling me you've never hit someone? Never beaten a customer who wouldn't or couldn't pay? Because if you are, I don't believe you.' As I said the words I realised just how true they were. I'd never looked at my opinions of Danny very closely before, afraid of what I'd find. But here it was – laid bare for all to see.

'You do realise people have been in there since the night of the storm?' He ignored my question and hit me with one of his own.

I thought about it. When did we bring up the last of the provisions?

'Connor! Come up here will you?' Danny shouted back towards the cockpit and I saw Carl take over the wheel.

'What's going on?' Connor asked when he arrived.

'Can you please tell mother dearest that you've been in the skipper's cabin since the night of the storm?'

Connor looked back and forth between the two of us, not quite sure what was going on. 'You mean since...'

'Yes, I do mean since Bella went missing,' Danny snapped.

Connor drew his brother a look. 'It's true, I have. I brought up the rest of the supplies a couple of days ago.'

'Thank you. There you go!' Danny said triumphantly.

'Can one of you please–'

'Our darling mother, seems to think I might have been the one to cut Bella's lifeline and then I somehow managed to get her into the skipper's cabin on the night of the storm, all in the space of ten minutes. Not to mention keeping her quiet for the last three days.' When Danny put it like that, I realised how ridiculous my theory was and I found I couldn't blame him for his bitterness.

'As much as I hate to say it, he's right.' Connor winced as he spoke.

How could I have forgotten Connor had been in the cabin? Did I think the rest of the food had somehow magically appeared in the galley? I tried to comfort myself by acknowledging we had been on a nightmare voyage and I was allowed to lose track of days and time. I'd be surprised if anyone could keep track with everything that had gone on.

'I'm sorry.' I murmured the apology and made my way back

along the boat. I found, yet again, that I just wanted to be alone. The closest I could get was my cabin, where Flick would at least be asleep.

I picked up my water bottle and book on the way past the table. Turning the handle on my cabin door as quietly as I could, I snuck inside. If Flick was still asleep, I wanted to avoid waking her at all costs. If she woke up I'd be forced to make conversation and that's the last thing I wanted.

I needn't have been worried though. Once inside, I could hear soft, muffled snores coming from Flick's side of the bed. I never could work out how she could sleep with her head under the covers like that.

I puffed up my pillows and leant against them, thinking I would go back to *In The Blink of An Eye*. I'd only managed a few pages, but it was shaping up to be a good book. I turned to the relevant page and began reading.

Despite my best intentions, I couldn't concentrate and eventually I gave up trying. I stared out of the small porthole beside me and watched the horizon bob up and down as *Duchess* moved with the swell.

There was one thing I couldn't get out of my mind. Obviously Danny hadn't attacked and kidnapped Bella. But that didn't mean he hadn't sliced though her lifeline and then pushed her overboard for the same reasons Erin had given me earlier.

I'd invited a killer on board.

CHAPTER THIRTY-THREE

THE NORTH ATLANTIC – DAY SIXTEEN

For two days I tried, and failed, to ignore the burning questions in my mind. Apart from wondering if one of my sons was capable of such a callous murder, I also couldn't stop thinking about whether whoever *had* killed Bella might do it again. I mean, what was to stop them? And although nobody said it out loud, I had to assume everyone else was thinking the same.

I tried any means possible to distract myself. Checking and rechecking the course on the charts was my favourite way to bore myself silly. We were so close to the Caribbean now, that even if we missed St Lucia somehow, we'd end up hitting one of the other islands; chart-checking was just busy work.

I continued announcing to anyone who'd listen how many miles there were until we arrived and it gave me a faint glow of hope. I saw a sliver of light penetrating my gloom that meant we would be off this boat, *safe*, very soon. I could also see the relief on my crewmates' faces every time they realised we were getting closer to the end of this living hell.

Reading charts soon left me with square eyes, so fishing, and wildlife watching became my go-to pastimes. I harboured hopes of catching a tuna fish and spotting a great white shark – from a distance of course – neither of which I'd managed before. The fish I did catch were greatly appreciated by everyone, since all of our fresh food had long since run out. Jonty cooked it up for us and we ate it with lemon juice from a bottle, sitting in the cockpit, absorbing as much sunshine as possible.

Occasionally someone joined me in my quest to catch us lunch, sometimes they were just nearby – company. Erin continued to either tap furiously at her keyboard, or scribble furiously in her notebook; neither was done slowly. People spent more and more time in the cockpit, less and less time in the saloon – the weather was glorious most of the time and no one wanted to be indoors if they could help it.

Overnight, nature treated us to one of its most spectacular shows – bioluminescence. Millions, *billions*, of plankton glowed all across the surface of the ocean, making it light up as if someone had cast a net of fairy lights across it. I had seen this incredible force of nature many times over the years, but each time I found myself pulled by it. Towards what, I could never tell, but it held me in its thrall and all mundane thoughts of life were chased from my mind.

I found myself appreciating the bigger world, the greater galaxy in which we all lived. These tiny, microscopic creatures, invisible to the naked eye even, could manifest something within themselves and light up an ocean so big, sailors wouldn't see land for days, weeks, at a time. Between the billions of stars lighting up the sky, even in the absence of the moon, and the plankton lighting up the sea, I felt like a tiny insignificant dot, and I was reminded of my own vulnerability.

During the day, when I wasn't on watch, or fishing, or sleeping, I checked the sat phone every few hours. A part of me still hoped for news of Bella, and if Hugo remembered, I wanted to be the first to know. Given everything that had happened since we left Gran Canaria I knew in my bones Hugo's attack was not a random act of violence.

We'd just finished the afternoon watch – midday to 6pm – and dinner wasn't quite ready. I took the sat phone up to the foredeck before we sat down in case there had been any messages in the last few hours. I didn't want anyone else around me if I had to hear bad news and I no longer cared what Danny thought of me going near the skipper's cabin. It was far too late to worry about any of that now.

After a few minutes, the satellites aligned and the handset chirruped to let me know I had a signal. I checked for messages, but to my continued disappointment there was nothing. I didn't know why I kept getting my hopes up. I knew Bella was gone and I knew it was unlikely Hugo would remember anything soon.

I sat on deck, with my arms resting on my bent knees and my head hanging between them. I was exhausted. And not the kind of exhausted you get from being at sea for over a month with weird sleep patterns and constantly changing time zones. It was the exhausted you get from too much responsibility, from too much happening around you that you try to, but can't, control. The exhausted that twelve hours of uninterrupted sleep would never cure.

I raised my head to the sky and as the wind rushed at my upturned face, I felt a wet coldness. I blinked my eyes open, expecting rain, although there'd been barely a cloud in the sky for days, dark or otherwise. I wiped at my cheek and realised I was crying, and the moment I did, I could no longer hold in the emotion. Sobbing, I allowed all the anger, resentment, disappointment, both at myself and everyone else, and crushing guilt to flow out of me.

I don't know how long I was there for, but once I'd finished, I was spent. However it was possible, I was even more exhausted than I had been before. Allowing myself the time to gather my wits, I readied myself to face the others. I could not show them I had been broken. Whatever had happened I was still in charge, responsible, and they still needed to rely on me to skipper *Duchess*. I owed them that at the very least.

The others had decided to eat at the table in the cockpit and I was grateful. For some reason, conversation wasn't an expectation when we ate outside. I picked at my food and tried to eat. Tried to take my own advice about acquiring all the energy you could get while you were trying to wrestle a yacht across the ocean.

I had long since zoned out of whatever conversation was going on around me. Instead, I was staring at the horizon; staring but not seeing. I'd often found the sea held many answers to whatever questions I had, but today it was letting me down. I stared harder.

'Helen? Helen!'

I felt someone hold onto my arm and I turned to look.

'Helen, are you okay?' Nick was peering at me.

'Yeah, miles away, sorry.'

'The sat phone was ringing.' Nick pointed to where Sean was holding it out to me. I hadn't bothered to put it away before we ate.

'Why did no one answer it?' I snatched the phone from Sean's hand and launched myself over the back of the seat, beyond caring if I left a footprint on the cushions.

I pushed at the accept button as I made my way to the front of the boat.

'Hello? Hello? Is there someone there?'

'He– Can you–'

'Hello? Yes, I'm here, can you hear me?'

'–at's better. Can you hear me?'

'Yes, yes, I can hear you now.'

'It's Sub-inspector Alcaraz.' The policeman investigating Hugo's attack.

'Hello. How is Hugo? Is he still okay?' Panic surged through me. It struck me in that moment that perhaps something terrible had happened to Hugo in the last couple of days. He'd relapsed, or had some kind of hidden blood clot that had silently killed him.

'Señor Marshall is fine, señora. He has remembered who pushed him down the stairs and he is certain it must be the same person who hit him on the head.'

I waited. Eyes screwed tightly shut, my lungs full of a held breath.

When Sub-inspector Alcaraz told me the name of the person Hugo said had attacked him, I asked him to repeat it. Several times.

Surely not?

CHAPTER THIRTY-FOUR

THE NORTH ATLANTIC – DAY SEVENTEEN

I woke up properly sometime around 10.30 on the morning of day seventeen. I'd been on the midnight watch until 6am with Erin and Nick, and then tried to sleep. Despite having been awake for almost a day, and feeling tired when I lay down, proper sleep was elusive. I tossed and turned, snatching thirty minutes here, and ten minutes there until I finally gave up. Sleep was overrated and if my body truly needed it, it could have it on dry land in a couple of days.

Yesterday Sub-inspector Alcaraz had given me the name of the person Hugo believed had attacked him and I still couldn't believe it. I hadn't shared that information with any of my crewmates, fobbing them off with non-answers, and neither had I confronted the person in question. The policeman had told me he was in contact with officers in St Lucia and Hugo's attacker would be brought in for questioning as soon as we arrived on the island.

I told myself to let the police deal with it. I told myself confronting them would serve no useful purpose. But then I thought about Bella; what if it was the same person who pushed her overboard? Shouldn't I shine a light into the dark corners of this nightmare so that everyone else could be safe? Forewarned is forearmed and all that.

But then, I thought, what if everyone turned on them? I knew my imagination was working overtime, but we had been stuck in something like 800 square feet of space with eight or nine other people for weeks, with little respite. When you added to it that this had been a nightmare journey, it wasn't a stretch to suggest tempers could fray. Or snap.

And then there was the fucking huge elephant on board. The stonking great pile of cocaine in the skipper's cabin. Yes, Danny's... *friends* were due to pick it up in a day or so, but knowing the police would be meeting us in the harbour made me feel uneasy. If nothing else, I needed to tell Danny so that he wouldn't panic when he saw them, and end up doing something stupid. The police in St Lucia had guns.

I had a wash and brushed my teeth – thank God for en-suite heads – and then opened my bunk door. I guessed Erin and Nick were still sleeping since they'd been on the midnight watch with me. Flick, Jonty and Sean were on watch, and I didn't even want to think about what Carl and Danny might be up to, but they were nowhere to be seen either. Connor was curled up in a corner of the bench, reading, one half of the book curved behind the other. Erin would have a fit if she caught him with it like that.

'Get you anything?' I asked as I wandered into the galley.

'Hmm?' He didn't look up, I waited. 'Oh, no ta.'

I made myself a coffee and then went to sit with Connor. He was the only person on board I trusted entirely and as much as I wanted to talk to him, he was still just a kid really. Too young to be given the kind of responsibility and pressures having this kind of conversation would give him.

'Okay?' he asked, dragging his eyes from the text and smiling.

I smiled back. 'Yeah, fine,' I replied in what was hopefully a breezy and light manner.

I let Connor go back to his book, while I sipped at my coffee and returned to my thoughts. God! I was so sick of *thinking* all the bloody time. I needed to *do* something.

There was one thing I could do right now. And that was tell Danny the police were meeting us in St Lucia. I had to make sure, for all our sakes, that his hoard would be off *Duchess* in plenty of time. I had this terrible fear that for some reason the police might just show up in a launch, rather than waiting for us to berth alongside. I just hoped he wouldn't force me to tell him who Hugo's attacker was.

I persuaded Danny to come up to the bow to talk to me without Carl in tow. I swear those two had become joined at the hip. I didn't know who was the worse influence; I suspected Danny, but Carl was not my responsibility, not in that sense anyway. Carl could get involved in whatever he wanted, as long as it didn't affect me, or my friends and family.

I refused to acknowledge the pecking thought that Danny *was* family.

'Well, isn't this all very cloak and dagger?'

I really wished he'd take things a bit more seriously sometimes.

I stared at him for a moment, willing him to get the message. 'There's something I need to tell you.'

'Oh, even more intriguing!'

'Danny, this is fucking serious, all right? Stop messing around.'

'Yes, Mum.'

Jesus, he made me want to slap him sometimes.

Suddenly, now the time was here, I found I didn't have the words. Or rather, I did, but I didn't know what order to speak them in.

'Well?' Danny caught my attention by snapping his fingers. He knew it was a sure-fire way to bring my temper to the surface, and it worked.

'The police are meeting us when we arrive in St Lucia.' I

deliberately didn't give him all of the information and I took guilty delight in watching his thoughts and emotions play out across his face.

Danny took a step towards me – aggressive. I couldn't help but flinch.

'What have you said?' he snarled.

'I haven't told them anything,' I replied, my chin jutting forward – equally aggressive.

'You must have. Why else would they be meeting us off the boat?' He grabbed my arm.

'Because Hugo remembered.' I wrenched my arm free, but he wasn't holding on so tightly anymore and I stumbled.

When I found my footing I looked up and Danny was glaring at me.

'No need to worry, it's not you they're after.' It was childish and for a moment I regretted toying with him.

'If Hugo's remembered, and the police are coming to the harbour to meet us, then that means whoever attacked Hugo is on this boat.'

I didn't offer any response, just stared at him.

'Do you know who it is? You do, don't you? Tell me!' The aggression was back, fiercer than ever.

'You don't need to know.' I realised as I said it, I'd made a mistake. There was no way Danny was going to let this go. I shouldn't have let on I knew. I shouldn't have said a *word*, but I needed to be sure the drugs were off the boat in plenty of time. I couldn't risk anyone else getting into trouble because of me and my poor choices.

'Don't need to know? Every person on board has a right to know. They have a right to know who they need to protect themselves from.' Danny turned and made his way back to the cockpit. I scrambled after him.

When I stepped down into the cockpit, he was shouting down through the hatch.

'You guys need to get up here, now. My dearest mother has something to tell you all!'

Jonty, Sean and Flick were watching me with curiosity from where they were chatting behind the wheel.

'What's going on?' Flick asked.

'Mum knows who attacked Hugo, and they're on this boat.'

CHAPTER THIRTY-FIVE

With the exception of Jonty, who was steering, we were now all sitting around the table in the cockpit. From my seat I could see Jonty's focus alternating between keeping an eye on the sea and making sure he didn't miss what was going on.

Six pairs of eyes were watching me, greedy for information. One pair stared at their hands, and I couldn't believe nobody had worked it out yet.

'You really know who attacked Hugo?' Nick asked gently. It felt like he was trying to ease me in, give me an opening.

'Yes.' My voice broke as if it hadn't been used for a while. I tried again. 'Yes, I do–'

Flick cut in. 'Then you need to tell us. We have a right to know.'

'That's what I said,' Danny agreed.

I noticed a couple of people glance his way, surprised, their looks telling me Erin wasn't the only one who suspected him.

I lifted my hands from the table where they lay and held them palms forward. 'Just... stop a sec. I will tell you,' I saw a mixture of anger and fear in the eyes of those around me, '*but* before I do, let's bear in mind, Hugo's memory may not be quite right and nothing has been proven yet. I don't want anybody giving this person a hard time. It's a matter for the police.'

I waited, watching.

'Do I have your agreement?' Most people nodded. 'Sean?'

He didn't say anything for a few seconds, but then, 'Fine.'

I took a deep breath and looked skywards, my mouth was suddenly dry. I sipped some water and tried again.

'Hugo remembers seeing–'

'It was me. Hugo remembers seeing me.'

There were gasps, and the word 'no' was breathed out by Flick and Nick. I confess to being relieved I hadn't had to say Erin's name out loud.

'*You?*' Danny couldn't believe it either. I suppose in his world it really never is the quiet ones.

'But why? Erin wouldn't hurt a fly!' Flick's voice was shrill.

Everyone began talking at once, speaking over one another and Erin didn't have the opportunity to reply. They bombarded her with questions and accusations. She looked overwhelmed and although I had little sympathy for her, I did believe she was entitled to tell her side of the story; to defend herself, although I couldn't imagine what she could say that would condone what she'd done.

She shrank into herself, shoulders up and arms folded protectively across her chest. It was weirdly incongruous to see her sitting like that, but yet with the hot sun on her shoulders and sunglasses hiding her eyes.

After a minute or two – I wasn't inclined to let her off too easily – I banged my hands on the table and shouted for everyone to be quiet.

'Can everyone just stop for a second. I know you all have questions and demand answers, me too, but you have to let Erin speak. And she can't do that while you're all firing word cannons at her.'

Erin sent me a thank you with her eyes, I pretended I hadn't seen. Right now, she was just someone who happened to be on board with us. I'd analyse how I felt about not really knowing my friend at all, and inviting someone like her to a place where trust was paramount, later.

'Thank you, Helen.' Erin's voice was just loud enough to be heard above the wind. 'I-I… it was an accident. I never meant to hurt him, I just wanted him to stop.'

'Stop what?' Flick interrupted.

'He was… he was coming on to me and he wouldn't stop. You remember what he was like in the bar. I knew he was just drunk, but I was scared. It was dark there was no one else around and… I suppose I panicked.'

'But you were in the marina, if you'd screamed, loads of people would hear you.' Nick's confusion was apparent.

'Yes, but I… Look it's difficult to explain, I wanted him to stop, but I didn't want people to think badly of him. Like you said, Flick, he wouldn't hurt a fly, he was just pissed and being stupid. I knew he would regret it in the morning, but in that moment, I just needed him to stop.' The words poured from Erin in a torrent. She paused and took a breath. 'I didn't realise how close we were to the steps when I pushed him, and then he fell.' Erin covered her mouth with her hand and whimpered. 'It was an accident, I promise. I only pushed him and he fell down the stairs. I ran off after that. I never meant to really hurt him.'

I watched, open-mouthed, as Erin covered her face to hide her tears. I couldn't believe it.

'Why didn't you say anything? Call an ambulance? If it was an accident, surely you would have at least called an ambulance.' Sean peppered her with questions.

Erin swiped at the tears on her cheeks before she replied. 'I didn't call an ambulance because I didn't know the number and I didn't have my phone.'

'That's no excuse, you could have woken one of us when you

got back. Or at least told us what had happened and we could have made sure he was okay,' Sean shouted.

'I panicked. I didn't think anyone would believe me. You were all friends with him and none of you know me, why would you believe me? I thought he'd just sleep it off and then make his way back to the boat.'

'You helped look for him.' Sean was stoney-faced. I'd never seen him so serious.

'I know, and I should have said something then. I'm sorry. I tried to think of a way to somehow get over to that side of the marina, but everything I thought of seemed so contrived.'

'What were you even doing over there so late at night anyway?' Connor asked.

'I went for a walk. I can't sleep on this bloody thing and I already wanted to be off it for as long as possible.' The tension in Erin's expression and her spitting tone were startling. It can be hard to get used to living and sleeping in constantly moving close quarters, but I hadn't expected the vehemence.

When she next spoke she had amended her tone. 'It took me ages to get used to being on board. It's not so bad now, but back in Gran Canaria it was awful and I took the opportunity to be on dry land as often as possible.'

'I can't believe you just left him there. Even if it was an accident–'

'It was!'

'That doesn't excuse you leaving him there. You could have at least told us the next morning when we realised he wasn't on board. I'm glad you're on someone else's watch and I don't have to rely on you to watch my back.' Sean stood and climbed over the bench. He took the wheel from Jonty with nothing more than a nod.

Erin was adamant she had only pushed Hugo, but the police said he'd also been hit on the head – hard, which was worrying.

CHAPTER THIRTY-SIX

THE NORTH ATLANTIC – DAY EIGHTEEN

I didn't get the opportunity to talk to Erin until the following evening. We'd been on the midnight until six watch, but apart from being too tired, I couldn't think of a reasonable excuse to get rid of Nick.

As it was, luck was on my side. Nick had gone for a nap before dinner and woken late. I insisted he eat first, assuring him I would be fine on my own with Erin. She may have done an awful thing, but she was unlikely to do anything now everyone knew she was responsible for Hugo's injuries. Whether she was guilty of a crime or not, wasn't for me to decide, but I had questions for her.

Being alone on a boat of this size was hard, and I'd spent the whole day quietly fuming. Thoughts of a previous conversation cycled round in my mind and I'd practised what I wanted to say to her over and over again. It changed every time, but it had to come out. The compulsion was overwhelming, and I had no choice but to talk to her about it before she was taken away by the police, because after that I was sure I would never see her again. Actually, I was sure I never *wanted* to see her again.

'You feel safe enough to be alone with me then?' Erin said peevishly.

'Don't. I'm not pissed, or "coming on to you", remember?' I used my fingers to make air quotes, my scorn on show; clear for her to see.

She had the good grace to blush a little. I wasn't sure I believed her story, but I was sure the police would keep digging. My problem with Erin was a little closer to home.

'Why did you try and pin the blame on Danny?'

Erin looked startled.

'What? Did you think I'd forgotten about that conversation?'

Erin stared out to the water, as if gathering her thoughts. She was quiet for so long, I almost asked the question again.

'I'm sorry I accused Danny of attacking Hugo. Obviously I knew it wasn't him, but that doesn't mean he isn't responsible for Bella.'

'Tell me you're joking?' I couldn't believe it.

'It still makes sense, why he would want to get rid of her.'

'I don't believe you. Why would I? You've already lied.'

'Look, yes, I was case-building, or whatever you want to call it, but I still think it was Danny. Who else would have a motive?'

Her words pulled me up short. Not because I thought she was right, but because I'd forgotten. I'd forgotten that even though Hugo's attacker had been found out, Bella's hadn't. How quickly I'd moved on, compartmentalised. What was wrong with me?

'See, you know I'm right.' Erin had mistaken my silence for concurrence.

'I don't know who else could have a motive. I'd say no one, not even Danny, but then, I never thought you'd leave a man unconscious at the bottom of some stairs.'

'Oh, come on, Helen. Danny's bad news. You and I have both known it since he was young and he used to nick the other kids' dinner money.'

'There's a massive difference between nicking a few quid as a child, and pushing someone overboard in the middle of the Atlantic with virtually zero chance of rescue. I've no doubt Danny's done some nasty stuff, but I refuse to believe my son could be so... so callous.'

'Your son?' Erin laughed once. 'It's been a while since I heard you refer to him so lovingly.'

She was right. But I was still his mother and it was still my job to defend him where I thought he was being unfairly disparaged. I was more than willing to accept all of Danny's true negative points, but if I thought someone was being unfair towards him, the mama bear inside me still existed.

'Yes, he's still my son, even if I don't agree with some of the things he's done.'

'*Some* of the things. The man's a drug dealer and a pimp. He gets prostitutes hooked on his drugs, makes them go out to work for him *and* charges them for the drugs he plies them with.' Erin threw the words at me before her hand flew to her mouth. Her eyes wide.

It was a sucker punch. Erin's words knocked the wind out of me, just as if she had jabbed me in the stomach with her fist. *Prostitutes. Pimp.* I stared at her, aware I was goggle-eyed and fish-mouthed.

'Oh, didn't you know about the whores?' she asked, recovering quickly and owning her impetuousness. Faux innocence coming off her in waves.

'I don't believe you. How would you even know?'

Erin only had to say one word and suddenly everything started falling into place.

'Rhea.'

I stared at her, unsure what she was not saying. Or at least unwilling to accept it. 'You don't mean...'

Erin nodded softly.

'But you told us she...'

'I told you she suicided because I couldn't bear the shame.

Depression is something people understand these days; being a sex worker isn't. She actually took an accidental overdose. I couldn't stand to see the sympathy on your faces when all the while you'd be condemning her in your minds and behind my back. But it wasn't her fault; it was his.' Erin stabbed a finger towards the lower deck, towards Danny.

'I don't understand. How did,' I paused, 'she end up on the streets?'

'You mean, how could I let it happen? That's what you really want to ask, isn't it?'

'No, that's not what I meant. I know you and Rhea had a... strained relationship, but she was an adult. She could make her own choices. I just can't understand why she would choose to sell her body.' The thought sent a shiver through me, despite the warm sunshine.

'That's the whole point though, isn't it,' Erin said bitterly. 'It wasn't a choice. That's what I'm telling you. Rhea and Danny have known each other since they were kids. Rhea needed help; Danny offered her help. Except it wasn't the kind she needed, but she took it anyway. He gave her free drugs and then once she was addicted, he started demanding payment. When she couldn't pay, he forced her onto the streets, and to face what those vile men were doing to her, she needed more drugs.'

'Erin, I'm so sorry.'

'I don't want your sorries, Helen. I want Danny to pay for what he did to Rhea, and what I'm certain he did to Bella.' Erin's vengeful tone made the hairs on my arms stand up.

'Is that why you agreed to come with us?'

'What? No, of course not. Danny wasn't even supposed to be here, remember. This was genuinely an opportunity for me to get away, move on and try to write something again.'

I began clutching at straws. 'Did you hurt Hugo knowing that I'd ask Danny to help? Is that why you left him?'

'No! That really was an accident. I was furious, though, when

I found out you'd allowed him to use *Duchess*, use *us*, to smuggle drugs.'

'I didn't have a choice; he's my son. I had to help him,' I said quietly. Now I understood why she was angry with me, it made sense, it really did, but how was I to know about Rhea? She never told us the truth; she couldn't be indignant about something when she deliberately kept us in the dark. Besides, I had my own skin, and my own child, to think about, and I told her so.

'I can't believe you're defending him. Would it have made a difference? If you'd known about Rhea and what your *son* did to her, would it have stopped you?'

I grew still and forced myself to think about it. *Would* I have? I weighed it up, the chance to get almost debt free and keep my son alive, versus Erin's peace of mind.

'Exactly.'

'I—'

'You didn't need to say a word, it's written all over your face.'

Attack is the best form of defence. 'Can you blame me? You know Big Malky; he isn't a man to mess around with. He made it perfectly clear how much he expected, and what he'd do to me if I didn't pay up when I got home. Your comfort, versus my life – no contest. And I wasn't about to trade Danny's life either.'

It was brutally harsh, but it was the truth.

CHAPTER THIRTY-SEVEN

THE NORTH ATLANTIC – DAY NINETEEN

The rest of the watch passed in virtual silence. At first, Nick tried hard to keep a conversation going, but soon gave up. Not only could I not stand the questions, no matter what Erin had done, I wasn't cruel enough to lay her pain bare. She could explain it, or not, it was her choice.

The following morning, Erin's revelation about Rhea played heavily on my mind. I wanted to ask her more questions, delve deeper into what had happened and Danny's part in it, but I was angry with her and I knew she was angry with me too. I wasn't sure we could have a conversation without causing more upset and tension.

There was another reason too. Today was the day Danny's 'mates' were due to come and meet us. I'd been on watch until midnight the night before, but I'd still woken just before dawn and couldn't get back to sleep. Instead, I dressed and made my way up on deck with a pair of binoculars.

Sunrises in this part of the world were almost always spectacular, but this morning the sky turned a particularly vibrant shade of red as the sun appeared over the horizon. I was reminded of the old saying, *Red sky at night, sailors' delight. Red sky in the morning, sailors' warning.*

It felt like an ominous hint at something menacing to come. A breeze drifted over the deck and I shivered, whether because of the sudden gust or because someone had walked over my grave, I couldn't tell.

I used the binoculars to check for other vessels. I knew the drugs weren't due to be collected until later in the day, but I couldn't help being paranoid about a coastguard ship or maritime police sneaking up on us. There's no reason why they should have; and we were still too far out, but after the luck we'd had so far, I didn't want to take any chances.

A while later I'd nearly bored myself silly with scanning an empty ocean and asking myself 'what-if' questions constantly. I'd managed to do quite the job of distracting myself, but between the boredom and my rumbling stomach it was time to face people.

I nodded at Connor, Danny and Carl on the way down to the galley; none of them seemed to be talking to each other either. Down below, Erin and Nick were sitting at opposite ends of the table. Nick staring straight ahead, one hand holding a cup still set on the table. Erin was, as usual, typing on her laptop.

Something broke inside me.

'Seriously? After what's gone on, you're still writing? What kind of person can still work after *everything* that's gone on in the last few days. After everything we've talked about.' I shook my head. 'You're not human.'

Erin stopped typing, but didn't remove her hands from the keyboard. Her mouth was slightly open as if she wanted to speak, but didn't quite know what to say. Eventually, she closed her laptop and retreated to her cabin having not said a word.

I threw up my hands. 'For fuck sake.'

'What did you expect her to say, Helen?' Nick asked quietly.

'Don't you go defending her,' I said, fiercely. 'I know you two had some kind of thing going on, but even you must–'

'There was no *thing*. I liked her, yes, but things change. I know you're angry with her and I understand why, but having to defend herself constantly must be exhausting.'

'Well, maybe she should just stop trying. What she did was indefensible.'

'But she has stopped!'

I paused. He was right, but I wasn't about to admit it. 'Whatever. When we get off this boat, I never want to see her again.'

'She's your friend.'

'No – she *was* my friend.'

Nick raised an eyebrow before picking up a book from the shelf and opening it. He had nothing more to say on the matter.

I clattered around the galley making a coffee. Emotions collided within me, making me jittery and anxious. Anger, worry, nervousness, betrayal, protectiveness and a little bit of fear. Who pushed Bella overboard? Would we get away with smuggling drugs?

By the time Danny's drug-dealer mates turned up I just wanted it to be over. I no longer cared if we were caught or not; one way or another I'd have one less thing to worry about in a couple of hours. I tried to imagine the relief I would feel, but it wouldn't come.

I'd had no part in the arrangements. Nor did I want to know the details. Danny organised everything using a sat phone he'd brought along himself. All I cared about was the date and time. Of course, being at sea, the time was always approximate.

I'd been so uninterested in the details, it hadn't even occurred to me to wonder what kind of boat they would be in. But I wasn't surprised when I saw a twenty-four-foot bay boat coming across the ocean towards us.

A bay boat made perfect sense. Not only could you fish, or

land, in shallow waters but they were stable enough to handle deep water too. Just the kind of boat you needed to pick up drugs out at sea and then land on an out-of-the-way beach somewhere far from law enforcement. Using the binoculars I could see three men on board: one was standing under the canopy, driving and the other two stood menacingly in front.

Mind you, I'd look pissed off if I'd been stuck on a boat that size for hours too. Although the bay boat was a lot quicker than *Duchess*, and they hadn't travelled all the way from the other side of St Lucia, where we were headed, their journey would still have taken several hours. And they were only halfway done.

As the smaller boat came alongside, I was suddenly frightened. What if they tried to take over the boat? Kidnap us for a ransom? What if the drugs weren't enough for them?

I moved towards Danny to seek his reassurance, but as I began to speak he cut me off.

'Not now, Mum.' He kept eyes on the men at all times and it occurred to me, he might be scared too.

'Get everybody up on deck, now,' I said to Nick who was standing next to me. I might be scared, but we outnumbered them and a show of numbers might, *might*, make them think twice. If nothing else it would make me feel better. I asked Flick to man the helm, I wanted all the boys available – just in case.

Those of us not involved stood together, watching and waiting for it all to be over. All apart from Erin – who had brought her laptop upstairs – but only after being told I'd ordered it. She was sitting in the cockpit at the table; even now she was still typing.

I gritted my teeth and turned away from her. In a little over twenty-four hours she wouldn't be my problem anymore.

We watched as Danny and Carl set to work. Carl in the skipper's cabin handing the packages up to Danny, who then passed them on to the smaller boat.

'You know, this would go a lot quicker if we had some help,' Danny called over to us.

No one moved. I wasn't about to ask, or order, anyone to do something that could, potentially, land them with a conspiracy charge in a foreign country. We were already too close to that as it was.

'He's right.' Sean scrambled over the deck and joined Danny. Connor followed and together they made a human chain to get the drugs off our boat quicker.

I caught Nick and Jonty looking at each other out of the corner of my eye. 'It's your choice. I've made mine.' And I stayed where I was.

In the end Nick and Jonty stayed where they were as well. The four men on *Duchess* and the two on the bay boat made short work of transferring the illicit cargo.

After it was done, and we'd waved them off with a sigh of relief, I caught hold of Danny. 'No one helped you.'

'What?' He tried to shrug out of my grasp, but I dug my fingers in further, emphasising my point.

'If we get caught, Sean and Connor did not help you. I don't care what you say about me or Carl, but you leave Sean and Connor out of it.'

'Whatever.'

I stood and watched the bay boat until it disappeared over the horizon before I moved. I wanted to make sure it really was gone and wasn't likely to come back.

The relief was mild, but I concentrated on the fact that in just over twenty-four hours, we would tie up in St Lucia.

And it would all be over.

CHAPTER THIRTY-EIGHT

Watches had become flexible and somewhat lackadaisical. I didn't like it and I wouldn't normally allow or encourage it, but we were so close to St Lucia, it hardly mattered. I did, however, insist, that the midnight and 6am watches were planned before anyone went to sleep.

After the drug dealers left with their stash, Flick had said she was fine to stay at the helm and Jonty and Connor said they would join her. I'd lost track a little bit, but I was sure it was Danny and Carl's turn to be on watch. It annoyed me they were so happy to let the others get on with it. But with three willing volunteers, it wasn't worth the argument.

Downstairs, I took my seat at the chart table and tried to distract myself by working out exactly how long it would be before we were in St Lucia, and I could get off this fucking boat. I'd never noticed before just how much I relied on the charts and the table to be my safe space.

The only noise in the saloon, was Erin's incessant tapping on her laptop. I tried to ignore it. I knew if I could distract myself for long enough, it would fade into the background and I wouldn't be aware of it anymore.

But no matter how hard I tried to immerse myself in my calculations, each and every tap was like a machine gun going off in the quiet around me. I closed my eyes and took a deep breath, reminding myself this was a communal space and she was perfectly entitled to write sitting at the saloon table if she wanted to.

The tapping stopped and I opened my eyes. Erin was peering at her screen intently, reading whatever was on there. I took the opportunity to try and lose myself in my calculations once more, taking advantage of the quiet time I'd been gifted.

Not even sixty seconds later, the machine-gun, rapid-fire tapping started all over again.

'Do you have to?' I snapped.

Erin flinched at the interruption and looked over, before sharing a look with Nick who was sitting at the other end of the table.

'Do I have to what?'

'Type so... *incessantly*. I can't hear myself think with your constant tap, tap, tapping. It's driving me crazy!'

'Um... sorry?' Erin glanced Nick's way again.

'What are you looking at him for? And how can you even write? I mean, doesn't all the stress and trauma we've gone through stop your brain from working?'

'No... it kind of makes it easier, actually.'

'Well, I think it's downright rude and disrespectful.'

'What?'

'Helen, I think you're going a bit far.' Why did Nick always have to defend her?

'I don't.'

'Do you think I should be morose, like you?' Erin spat.

'Morose? Is that your way of trying to show off? Show you're more intelligent than everyone else because you can use big words?'

'That's not what I was doing. Look, if it makes you happy, I'll stop.'

'Oh, so you can stop because I've called you out, but knowing one of our crewmates is dead in the sea somewhere somehow spurs you on?'

Nick and Erin gasped. Maybe I had gone too far, but it was basically what she said.

'What's going on?' Danny opened the door to his cabin from where he lay in his bunk and leaned out, rubbing the sleep from his eyes.

'Nothing,' I said, trying to shut the whole conversation down.

'Didn't sound like nothing,' replied Danny.

'Your mum thinks me writing my book is in some way disrespectful to Bella.'

Danny snorted. 'What are you writing about anyway?'

'It's a new book.'

'I hope you weren't inspired by us lot. Mind you, you write chick-lit don't you? Not a lot of romance going on here.'

Erin bristled and I felt a tug of cruel satisfaction. Erin hated her work being called chick-lit, said it demeaned a whole, very popular, genre. Normally I would agree with her, but I wasn't inclined to intervene on her behalf. She could defend herself; I wasn't about to do it for her, not anymore.

'Actually, I'm writing a crime novel this time,' Erin said superciliously.

'They do say a change is as good as a rest.' Danny was smirking and I knew he was having a dig at Erin's recent lack of success. My son might be a thug, but he could be clever when he wanted to be.

Erin had closed her laptop during their exchange and instead began writing in her notebook. I was surprised she hadn't filled it up already; she'd been scribbling away in it since before we left Scotland.

Danny climbed down from his bunk and sat at the table

beside Nick wearing just a pair of shorts. There was something in his eyes I recognised from when he was a child, and I knew he hadn't finished with Erin yet. Remembering what Erin had told me about Danny and Rhea, a wave of anxiety passed over me.

'Are you going to let us read it?'

'No!' Erin placed her hands protectively over her laptop. Was that fear etched across her face?

'You know we'll read it at some point, right? When it gets published, we can just buy it and read it.'

'That's different. No one reads my first draft apart from my editor.'

Nick and Danny were watching Erin, waiting for I don't know what. I was watching Danny, because I knew the next move would be his. I'd seen Erin like this before; she just wanted to shut down the conversation and let that be an end to it.

I was ready for it, but couldn't get out from behind the chart table quickly enough when it happened.

Danny launched himself across the length of the table, grabbing for Erin's laptop and said, 'Oh, go on!'

Erin jerked backwards, clutching her laptop, so quickly she banged her head on the wall. 'Ow!' Her chin wobbled and her eyes filled; whether she was scared or hurt, or both, I wasn't sure.

Nick was on his feet a second later, his arm thrust out in front of Danny.

'Danny, leave it,' I said.

'What? I was only messing around.'

'I said no! Why can't you just take no for an answer?' Erin was standing with her back against her cabin door now, furious, the laptop clutched tightly to her chest. I knew she wasn't just talking about her book now. And by the look on Danny's face, so did he.

'Sometimes, no just means, persuade me.' Danny's face was dark and sinister, despite the bright Caribbean sunshine flooding through the windows.

Erin blanched. 'Fuck off, and leave me alone!' She turned and threw open the door to her cabin, slamming it behind her.

It had started off being amusing, watching Danny wind up Erin, but now I felt sick. I'd seen an insight into the man he had become and, to be honest, it scared me.

Danny was staring at Erin's door and Nick's stare at me cut across his line of vision. He widened his eyes, silently urging me to do something to release the tension.

'Danny, can you go and relieve Flick, please. She's been up there for hours.'

Danny either didn't hear me, or was ignoring me.

'Danny!'

'What?'

I moved from behind the chart table and held onto his arm, tugging until he looked at me. 'Put some clothes on and go and relieve Flick. It's your turn.'

I waited for him to argue with me, but instead he went into his bunk space. After pulling on a top and some deck shoes, he went up on deck without another word.

Nick and I both sank into the sofa and let out heavy, relieved breaths as the atmosphere dropped around us.

CHAPTER THIRTY-NINE

THE NORTH ATLANTIC – EARLY HOURS OF DAY TWENTY

I should have known that wouldn't be the end of it.

Whether I was deluded, compartmentalising or unwilling to acknowledge the final few hours on board would be anything but straightforward, I couldn't tell you. But I can tell you, if you'd asked me what else might go wrong on this trip, I could've guessed a thousand things and what actually happened wouldn't have been amongst them.

Flick and I were woken by a pounding on the door around 3am. I could hear Danny yelling at us to get up, that we needed to see something. Flick and I groaned our way out of bed. Normally being woken in the middle of the night meant some kind of emergency, but the fact we didn't spring out of bed showed just how normal 'emergencies' on board *Duchess* had become.

We dressed and made our way into the saloon where we found Danny with a laptop in front of him. He was leaning on the table, his hands either side of the computer.

'Is that…?'

'Yep. Go upstairs, everyone needs to hear this together.'

'Up…? It's the middle of the night. What's going on, Danny?'

'You'll see in a minute. *Go* upstairs.'

I threw my arms in the air and followed Flick upstairs to the cockpit. It was a clear night and millions of stars twinkled above us. However, the lack of moon meant the only light was coming from down below through the hatch. It cast odd shadows on those of us sitting nearest; those sitting further away were in virtual blackness.

Nick and Erin had been on watch with Danny, but Carl, Jonty and Connor were there too. I took a seat beside Connor just as Sean appeared through the hatch rubbing sleep from his eyes.

'Does anyone know what's going on?' Jonty asked. All I could really see of him were the dull whites of his eyes.

Those of us who had just woken up, grunted in the negative.

'Do you two know what's happened?' I asked Nick and Erin, my voice still low and thick with sleep.

I could barely see Erin, but it was enough to know she wasn't looking at us. Nick replied for them both. 'He just said he was going to use the head and asked us if we wanted anything. About ten minutes later I heard him banging on doors, and then everyone started coming up the stairs.'

'*Ten* minutes? Did you not wonder where he was?'

'Well yeah, but I just figured he wanted a peaceful number two,' Nick replied.

There wasn't really any response to that. It wasn't uncommon; night-time was the most private time to use the head and if you had three people on watch, then why not?

I was nervous though. The laptop I'd seen Danny with downstairs was Erin's and it looked like he'd managed to gain access. Part of me wanted to go down and demand he tell me what was going on before he said anything to the rest of the crew, but I knew my son. Once he'd made his mind up, that was it. Whatever he was about to tell us had come from Erin's laptop and with a sinking heart I realised the drama on board was far from over.

Finally, Danny came upstairs with the laptop in hand. He

placed it on the table, still open, and stood at the head of the table like some kind of crime don.

'What the hell are you doing with my laptop?' Erin flung herself from behind the wheel and tried to get to Danny. Nick grabbed the wheel, while she was stopped from going any further by Carl.

She fought him viciously, trying to scratch at his face and wrenching her arms from his grasp. Until she stopped, suddenly, burying her face in her hands. Connor stood up and gently guided Erin into the vacant seat. She'd begun sobbing quietly, keening like a mewling cat.

I'd had enough.

'Danny, what the fuck is going on and why do you have Erin's laptop?' The surprised faces around me nodded in agreement.

'Yeah mate, just spit it out, will you?' Sean said.

Danny stood tall and made eye contact with each of us in turn. When he came to Erin he simply stared at the top of her head.

Just as I was about to snap at him again, he spoke.

'It was her.'

'What was? We know about Hugo.'

'No – I mean it was *all* her.'

My stomach writhed as I understood his meaning and I had to swallow to clear my throat in order to speak.

'Bella?' I whispered.

Danny nodded once, his eyes never leaving Erin.

'That's ridiculous,' said Nick from behind the wheel. 'She wouldn't…'

'Wouldn't she?'

'Look at her,' Nick said, and we did. 'She's a mess and that's just because you've invaded her privacy, gone behind her back and looked at her laptop. She doesn't have it in her to hurt anyone.'

'She hurt Hugo,' Sean interrupted.

'But that was an accident, wasn't it?' Flick asked, but the timbre of her voice betrayed that she was no longer sure.

'Not according to what I've read here,' said Danny. 'This book of hers seems to say she did it on purpose.'

'You read her book?' I don't know why I was surprised; he'd done much worse.

'Some of it, and her notes. Enough to know she's responsible for all the shit that's happened on board.' Danny spoke aggressively and if what he said was true, I didn't blame him.

'What the fuck, Erin?' Jonty said.

Erin pulled a tissue from her pocket and wiped her eyes. Everyone was staring, giving her a moment to compose herself before we demanded answers.

'I am *not* responsible for all the bad stuff that's happened on board.' She paused. 'I just wrote about it – *after* it happened.' We had to strain to hear her admission above the gentle breeze.

For a moment, no one said anything and then everyone spoke at once; shouting and spitting out questions. I pulled my thoughts together and tried to make them make sense.

'So you say,' replied Danny.

'It's true!' Erin shouted at him. 'Helen, you know me, you know I couldn't do this.'

I was already pissed off with Erin and her writing; it had felt disrespectful somehow. Now I was hearing she'd been writing about us the whole time? This was a whole new level of awful. Making a record of our misfortunes, of Bella's *death*, so she could sell a few books? I wouldn't have thought *that* of her, let alone murder. I knew I should be angry, but I didn't feel anything. I was numb.

I saw Danny say something to Carl, who then disappeared downstairs and I watched as Jonty spun Erin's laptop round to face him, the screen illuminating him from below, giving him a spooky Halloween face.

'How did you get in?' I asked Danny, nodding to the laptop.

'Just watched when she typed in the password a couple of times.' Danny shrugged.

Erin had leant forward onto the table, her head on her arms and she was crying like a child. No one was comforting her. I didn't want to comfort her either and she was supposed to be my friend.

'You're a fucking bitch. What kind of person writes about this shit? Just how callous are you?' I was reminded of the Flick from Clyde Marina before we set off.

'I just... I just needed to write a book. I didn't think–'

'No, you did think; it was just that you only thought about yourself.' Flick spat her words at Erin.

Erin stood and hurried downstairs, pushing past Carl on his way up.

'Woah! Where the fuck is she going?'

'Let her go,' I said. 'I don't want to look at her anyway.' I noticed Carl was holding something in his hand. 'What's that?'

'It's the notebook Erin's been writing everything down in. I asked Carl to get it. I still don't believe she's not responsible,' Danny answered.

'I think you might be right,' Jonty said looking up from the screen, his face white.

CHAPTER FORTY

Jonty spun the laptop around and pushed it towards me.

'I found this other document in Erin's files. It's a list of "ideas" on how to cause drama on board.'

I held Jonty's gaze, trying to decipher what he was telling me and then dropped my eyes to the screen, and read. Jonty was right.

As I read I realised some of this stuff had actually happened in the last few weeks. There were a few innocuous things, like how to cause conflict between certain members of the crew, offering back-handed compliments and generally gossiping. But there was one particular "idea" that made me catch my breath when I read it.

Cause an allergic reaction.

'What the fuck?' I breathed, my hand on my chest. I looked up to Jonty watching me, he screwed his mouth into a line and nodded.

'What is it?' Flick tried to grab the laptop, but I held on to it.

'When Bella had that allergic reaction... It wasn't an accident. Erin planned it, she deliberately gave Bella a drink with cow's milk in it to see what happened.'

'Did she write about it?' Connor asked.

Everyone was watching me now, even Nick who should've been watching the ocean.

'The manuscript's still open,' said Jonty. 'You can flick between them, do a search.'

I navigated to the correct document, it was entitled *The Boat Trip*. I located the search function and typed in 'allergic reaction'. I clicked on the search button and waited.

There were half a dozen hits. I scanned through them as quickly as I could. With each section I read, I felt more nauseous. It was all here, written almost exactly as it had happened just a couple of weeks ago.

One particular sentence jumped out at me. I read it several times and the significance of it slammed home.

This was how I was going to know for sure if Erin had written about our bad luck after it had happened, or if she'd caused it in the first place.

'Connor, come with me.' I stood and we made our way to the stairs.

'Where are you going?' Danny demanded.

'Stay here. I'll be back in a minute.'

Downstairs, there was no sign of Erin. I assumed she was in her cabin, which was fine by me. I stopped at the galley and turned to speak to Connor.

'I'm going to search her cabin. I just need you to make sure she doesn't stop me, but don't hurt her.' Connor looked mildly affronted. 'I know you wouldn't, which is why I brought *you* with me, I just needed to say it out loud.'

'Okay. Doesn't mean I'm not angry too though.'

'I know that, son.'

Without bothering to knock, I opened Erin's cabin door and switched on the light. She was curled up in the corner of the bed, hugging the duvet to her chest with one arm and shielding her eyes while trying to see who had entered her room.

'It's me and Connor,' I said, knowing she'd recognise my voice.

'I know you think I'm a horrible, vile person. You don't need to rub it in anymore.' Her voice was thick with tears.

'That's not why I'm here.' I removed any emotion from my words. I couldn't deal with them right now and if I was right, Erin was dead to me anyway.

'Then why are you here? Can't you just leave me alone? In a few hours we'll be in St Lucia and you never have to see me again.'

'I know. And I don't plan to.' I opened the locker nearest to me and started rifling through it.

'Hey! What the fuck are you doing? That's my stuff!' Erin propelled herself towards me, but Connor took a step and cut her off.

I ignored her and carried on looking. It hadn't occurred to me before, but all of Bella's things were here too. As captain, it would be my responsibility to make sure her belongings were returned to her family. Now was not the time for sentiment though, so I pushed all thoughts of the future aside. I needed to concentrate on what was happening right now.

'Are you at least going to tell me what you're looking for?'

'No.'

I pulled a rucksack from the locker and dumped it on the bed. Erin stared at it; she was terrified. This was it, I knew it.

I opened the top of the rucksack and tipped it upside down, the contents tumbled out. The name on the inside confirmed it was Erin's bag I had in my hand and the yellow-and-white tube nestled amongst a pile of detritus confirmed my worst fears.

'How could you?'

Erin's face hardened. She had no way out now. Nothing she could say would convince me she wasn't involved.

'I have nothing to say.'

I stared at her, unable to believe this woman had been my

friend. *I* had invited her on board because I felt sorry for her and I wanted to help. It was *my* fault Bella's lifeless body was floating around in the vast North Atlantic Ocean somewhere.

I heard the rattle of footsteps on the stairs at the other end of the boat. I turned to see Jonty, Sean and Danny coming towards us. I held up the EpiPen for them to see. Jonty and Sean looked confused.

'It's Bella's EpiPen,' I said. 'Hidden in Erin's rucksack. That was the first time she tried to kill her.'

'It wasn't me!' Erin screamed.

'I don't believe you!' I screamed back. 'First thing in the morning I'll be contacting the coastguard and asking them to inform the police in St Lucia. You can stay in here until then.'

'I don't think that's a good idea,' Jonty said. I gave him a questioning look. 'We've already found one piece of evidence, there might be more. What if she tries to destroy it?'

'He's right,' said Danny. 'We could put her in the skipper's cabin? It's only for a few hours.'

'No – you can't! What if the boat sinks? I'll be trapped.' Erin looked terrified.

'The only way this boat might sink is if you carry out your plan to put a hole in it and you won't be able to do that from there.'

'What?' I wasn't sure I'd heard right.

'One of the other things on Erin's list of ideas was to sink the boat, along with cause a fire and a few other horrific things.'

'I can't...' Did I even know this woman at all? 'Danny's right, she can sit in the skipper's cabin until we arrive in St Lucia and then she's the police's problem.'

I left the boys to deal with it and made my way up on deck.

'What's going on?' Flick asked.

I placed the EpiPen on the table, in the middle of the shaft of light bursting up from the hatch.

'Is that Bella's EpiPen?' Carl asked, peering at it through the darkness.

Flick gasped. 'That's… awful!'

'I know. It looks like she made things happen so she could see how people would react. Then she wrote them all down and planned to sell her manuscript as a crime book.'

There was a scuffling noise followed by Erin shouting, and we turned to face the hatch.

'What's going on?' Sean asked from behind the wheel.

'We're making her stay in the skipper's cabin until we arrive in St Lucia. I don't want her messing with any other evidence there might be down there.'

It took four people to get Erin down into the skipper's cabin, and at one point I was convinced someone would end up overboard.

Once she was safely ensconced in her new cabin, I took the laptop downstairs and shut myself away in my cabin. I wanted to read everything.

CHAPTER FORTY-ONE

ST LUCIA

By the time we arrived in St Lucia the following afternoon, you could have told me you had seen incontrovertible evidence zombies were real and I would have believed you. After the nightmare journey from Gran Canaria and what I had read in Erin's 'book' it seemed anything could be made true – you only had to make it happen.

We docked in Marigot Bay on the leeward, or westward, side of St Lucia. It was known as a premier superyacht haven and not without reason. The complex was amongst the most luxurious in the Caribbean, which boasted not only the marina, but a complete resort and spa. It was also one of the most secure anchoring points in the area. The bay was in something of a hurricane hole, surrounded by mountains and with very little tide changes it was a safe harbour during storm season.

We were greeted by staff members on the pontoon as well as the police we had been expecting. The two young men from the marina, dressed smartly in knee-length white tailored shorts and white polo shirts with aqua-blue trim, stood awkwardly beside the police officers dressed in their blue and navy uniforms. I couldn't imagine they often greeted guests with law enforcement officers standing beside them.

The staff members introduced themselves as George and Rubin after they had helped us tie up alongside. We made sure the boat was secure before the two police officers requested to come aboard.

'Yes, of course,' I replied. 'You might want to take a seat; there are some things you need to know.'

We sat in the cockpit. I had my hair scraped up under a cap and my sunglasses on. Although it was only around twenty-five degrees, there was little wind and the sun was intense. I tried to keep it brief. The crew were hot, sweaty and desperate to get onto dry land after almost three weeks at sea – even if they were only going to the police station for the moment. It had caused an argument with Danny and Carl at first.

'I'm not hanging around for any policemen!' Danny had shouted.

'They'll think it's more suspicious if you disappear before they talk to you though,' I replied.

'I'm not going anywhere near a police station.' Carl had looked more scared than angry.

'If you're not on this boat and willing to give a statement when the police ask, they are going to wonder what you've got to hide. You answer their questions, tell them what they want to know and then that's it. You can jump on a plane to wherever you want to go.'

Eventually I had persuaded them I was right.

Somehow, the news about Bella being missing hadn't been relayed to the local police and not for the first time I cursed the laid-back ways of the Caribbean. As far as they were concerned they were only here to take Erin in for questioning over Hugo's accident.

Sergeant Campbell had instructed PC Grant to take notes while he asked questions, but as I told them the story of our crossing and then told them about the manuscript and 'notes' we had found on Erin's laptop, PC Grant slowly stopped writing; instead he stared at me, his eyes wide. I couldn't tell if they believed me or not – hell, I wasn't sure I could quite believe it, but they listened without interrupting, only asking questions when I was finished.

'Where is Miss Monroe now?' Sergeant Campbell glanced towards the hatch.

'She's down below in the saloon. We put her in the skipper's cabin after we found the EpiPen. We, uh, we thought she might try to destroy any more evidence there might be. But it didn't seem fair to keep her in there once we arrived.'

Sergeant Campbell raised his eyebrows. 'That was good thinking. And the laptop?'

'It's down below in her cabin, along with her other belongings.'

'We will need to take her things and conduct a search of the yacht.'

I nodded my understanding and then remembered I would need to explain all of this to the company who had paid me to deliver *Duchess*. I doubted they would be quite so understanding.

'We will also need each crew member to make a statement at the station. Can you give me their names and contact details?'

'Of course, do you need to speak to any of them now? Only they are desperate to get ashore and go for a proper shower.'

Sergeant Campbell read over PC Grant's notes, nodding as he did so. 'I have a few questions for them just now and then they can make their statements in a day or so. They'll need to surrender their passports for the time being. I will ask some of my colleagues to come and help to make things as quick as possible.'

'Are you going to arrest Erin?'

The policemen exchanged a look before Sergeant Campbell

said, 'Yes, I think in light of what you have told us, we have no choice.'

After that, things moved quickly. PC Grant radioed for more officers to attend and Sergeant Campbell made his way down below. He placed Erin under arrest for the attack on Hugo and for Bella's murder.

'You can't arrest me. I haven't done anything!' Erin was shouting, but I could see she was scared too. I would've been; being arrested anywhere outside of Europe was one of my worst nightmares.

Sergeant Campbell handcuffed Erin's arms in front of her and instructed her to take a seat while they waited for transport to take her to the police station. The rest of the crew were taken upstairs, one by one and asked what they knew of Erin's alleged crimes. I couldn't imagine their stories were all that different, but it made sense the police wanted to be thorough.

After the crew were questioned, they were asked to hand over their passports and allowed to take their wash bags – searched first of course – a towel and a change of clothes and make use of the showers. Everything else remained to allow for thorough and proper examination of what was now a crime scene.

I stayed on board and watched as one half of Bella's lifeline was placed in a bag; PC Grant's neat handwriting identified it. Erin's laptop, Bella's EpiPen and most of the contents of their cabin were also put into differently sized plastic bags and identified on the outside.

I leaned back on the sofa, suddenly exhausted; absolutely bone tired. *Duchess* and her crew were no longer my responsibility and I felt the weight lift from me as if it were physical. All I wanted to do now, was sleep. Actually, I wanted to eat and then sleep.

'Will you at least contact the British Embassy and tell them where I am and that I've been arrested?' Erin's whiny voice cut through my quiet half-doze.

I opened one eye and looked at her, considering.

'I suppose.' I sighed.

'Thank you.' She said it so earnestly I truly believed she was grateful.

I informed the nearest police officer I needed to go and make some phone calls and I would be back soon.

The phone call to the embassy would be the easy one. I also needed to contact *Duchess*'s owner and let them know their new yacht was a crime scene.

CHAPTER FORTY-TWO

ST LUCIA – DAY TWO

It was lunchtime the day after we arrived in St Lucia before the remaining *Duchess* crew could get together. We'd all showered, rested and given our statements at the station, where we'd been asked to remain on the island a while longer. It was less of a request and more of a statement; they still had our passports, so there was no way for us to leave anyway.

It felt like every member of the crew had asked me the same questions, so I decided it would be better if I told them all together. We'd agreed to meet for lunch in a nearby rum bar where we could get some green figs and salt fish and wash it down with Piton beer. God knew we could all use a drink.

The others were already sat around a table with a bucket of beers in front of them when I arrived. It was the first time a few of them had been early for anything, I noted dryly.

'Has everyone ordered food?' I was starving; it was a weird thing that happened to me after a long sail.

'Some of us have. Here's a menu,' said Connor passing me a laminated piece of card. I ordered from the server and popped myself a beer from the bucket.

I took a long slurp, aware all eyes were on me. Deliberately, I placed the bottle on the table in front of me, squarely on the beer mat, and sucked the remaining beer from my lips. I didn't know where to start.

'Is Erin still at the police station?' Flick was the first to speak.

'Yeah, it looks like she'll be there for a while. The British High Commission are sending someone over to look after her.'

'She won't go to jail here though, will she? They'll send her back to the UK, won't they?' Flick looked around for confirmation.

I shrugged. 'Sergeant Campbell told me she could be prosecuted in any country since we were in international waters when the crime was committed.' *When the crime was committed.* God, it sounded so cold and callous, but it was the only way I could say it without getting emotional. 'I think there will be a push to get her home and deal with her there.'

'What about Hugo? Won't the Spanish police want to prosecute her there?'

'I really don't know the ins and outs of it, and if I'm totally honest, I don't want to. I did my bit by contacting the consulate and now I don't really care what happens to her.' My contempt was obviously clear, because no one asked me any more questions about what was going to happen to Erin.

'I think,' Jonty said, exchanging glances with everyone, 'what we really want to know is why and how.'

'Yeah, why Hugo and Bella? And how did she manage to get away with it?' Nick interjected.

My gaze involuntarily switched to Danny and he caught it.

'Why are you looking at me? What's it got to do with me?'

'More than you realise.' I paused, considering, for a moment. 'Erin blamed you for her daughter's death.'

'Rhea?'

I nodded.

'But I haven't seen her since we were kids. It's got to have been years.' Danny thought for a moment. 'And didn't she commit suicide anyway?'

'Yeah, you told us she'd killed herself, Mum.' Connor agreed with his brother.

I was confused. Why would Danny lie about seeing Rhea? He wasn't shy about what he did to earn money. I fidgeted in my seat, unsure how to phrase what I wanted to say. He might not have minded talking about his job, but it was far from comfortable for me.

'You… you gave her drugs, Danny, and…'

'And what? And I've never *given* anyone drugs in my life. I know you don't like what I do,' he said looking around the table, 'and I know it makes the rest of you uncomfortable talking about it, but I do this to make money. I don't give that shit away for free.'

Danny was right. People were fidgeting in their seats and avoiding eye contact wherever possible. Why was it so difficult to say?

Because I was ashamed of my son, it was as easy as that. And also a little bit scared of how he might react if I said so in front of so many people.

'For fuck sake! Whatever it is, just say it. I think we're beyond being coy now, aren't we?'

I flinched and then steadied myself. He was right, I just needed to say it out loud.

'Erin thinks you got Rhea hooked on drugs, then forced her to… become a sex worker in order to pay for the drugs she then couldn't live without.'

Danny stared at me for a moment, and then burst out laughing.

There was nothing funny about what I'd just said, and no one else seemed to think there was either. Although I might've caught a smirk on Carl's face, but he took a sip of his beer before I could be sure.

'It's not funny, Danny. None of this is fucking funny.' Jonty's lips tightened, his jaw clenched.

'I'm sorry, you're right, it's not, but that story Mum just told is ridiculous.'

Everyone was now watching Danny, waiting for an explanation.

'Fine, okay. Since you all seem so interested, *this* is how it works. I *sell* drugs, to anyone who wants to buy them. *Sometimes* if the girls haven't got the cash, I offer them an... alternative. But I don't give drugs away for free; I don't force anyone into prostitution and I definitely haven't seen Rhea Monroe anytime in recent history. So – whatever weird story Erin had in her head about Rhea, it was nothing to do with me.' Danny relaxed back into his seat, his beer in one hand and a smug look on his face until a moment of realisation replaced it. 'Wait. Even if Erin believed her story, why attack Hugo and then kill Bella?'

'She was going to blame it all on you. She was going to tell the police you killed Bella because she threatened to tell the police about the drugs. Bella was... collateral damage. Erin didn't care who she had to hurt to have her revenge on you. She truly believed you'd be prosecuted here in St Lucia and would end up rotting away in a foreign prison.' I paused. 'Tell me the truth, have you really not seen Rhea?'

'Not that I know of. I'm sure I'd recognise her. Have you got a picture?'

I pulled my phone out of my pocket and navigated to Erin's Facebook page. Even now it was full of pictures of Rhea. I found one of her in a pub somewhere, holding a glass of prosecco and smiling straight into the camera. I turned it around to show Danny and he leaned across the table to get a better look.

'*That's Rhea?*'

The shock in his eyes told me all I needed to know.

'You recognise her now?'

'Yeah, but that's not how I remember her, which might

explain a little bit why I didn't recognise her. And she didn't say her name was Rhea, it was something boring, ordinary…' He thought for a minute. 'Jane! I'm sure she said her name was Jane.'

'So what happened to her?' Flick asked and I realised everyone else was invested in the story.

'She was already a druggie when she came to me, but she'd run out of money. She'd been caught shoplifting a few times to pay for the drugs, but she didn't want to risk getting put away. Someone had told her I could get her work.'

'Work? Is that what you call putting poor young girls on the streets?' Nick was disgusted by what he was hearing.

Danny shot him a look. 'I helped her out. She would've ended up on the streets anyway. Girls like that always do. At least with me they had someone who actually looked after them.'

'Looked after them? How is forcing them to be prostitutes looking after them?' Nick wasn't backing down.

'I never forced anyone to do anything. The girls were free to come and go as they pleased. I didn't need to scare them into staying, there was always another one waiting to take their place. This was *their* choice.'

'Hang on, if Rhea didn't commit suicide, then how did she die?' Connor asked.

'It was an accidental overdose and Erin believes Danny supplied the drugs that caused it.'

CHAPTER FORTY-THREE

We stayed around that table for hours. Eating, drinking and talking around and around the subjects of Erin, Rhea, drugs, prostitutes and revenge.

I explained how Erin had managed to get away with pushing Bella over the side of *Duchess* during the storm.

'Was it all down to chance? Sean's bad tummy, the storm, Bella being on watch?'

'Sort of. Bella being on watch was serendipity for Erin, all she had to do was orchestrate a way of getting Sean off deck for long enough. So she put something in his drink, knowing it would cause diarrhoea. All she had to do was wait until he disappeared into the head. She told Bella that Sean had asked her to cover while he was indisposed. It didn't take much for her to slice through Bella's lifeline and then push her over. After that, she snuck back downstairs and into her cabin. She must have been soaked through, but since she was alone in the bunk, no one was any the wiser.' I offered Sean an apologetic look. I felt sorry for him; it really hadn't been his fault.

'And this is all in that book of hers?' Nick was incredulous.

'Yeah, except she obviously didn't write herself as the

murderer, she changed that character to a man and called him Jimmy.'

I fully understood the shock around me. I'd felt the same when I first read it. One person had lost their life and two others had been unwitting patsies in something that had nothing to do with them. I would never understand why Erin had decided on this form of vengeance.

'But when did she come up with the plan? Was attacking Hugo a deliberate thing, knowing you'd ask Danny to take his place? Is that what she intended? Or was Hugo's accident really an accident and she came up with the idea in the space of a couple of days?'

I shrugged. 'Her manuscript wasn't clear on that point, but I think she intended for Bella to die when she spiked her drink with ordinary milk. That's why she hid the EpiPen. I don't think she knew about Danny's allergy.'

'I was convinced Danny, or one of his mates – maybe you Carl, sorry – had hurt Hugo just so that Danny could become part of the crew and could smuggle the drugs over.' Jonty was apologetic. I didn't think he ought to feel too bad, it wasn't outwith the realms of possibility.

Danny was stoney-faced and Carl didn't look too impressed either. What did they expect though? They weren't exactly blameless.

My phone rang, cutting through the tension. I looked at the screen. 'It's the police.' I stood and answered the call before taking a few steps away from the table to hear what was being said. I listened as Sergeant Campbell spoke and I stared at Danny. He caught me looking and stared back. I beckoned him over.

'Okay, thank you. Yes, I'll tell him.' I ended the call.

'What? What is it?'

'The police want to talk to you. They're on their way here. They said Erin has given them some information they need to discuss. Apparently they've tried to ring you a couple of times.'

'My phone's been on silent. I need to go – now.'

The Caribbean was not a place you wanted to be convicted of dealing drugs, let alone smuggling them – not as a foreigner anyway.

'Carl! We need to get out of here. The police are coming.'

'What about your passports?'

'I'll figure that out later.'

I watched as Danny and Carl ran from the bar. I didn't know where they planned to go or how they planned to get away. The police had asked me not to tell Danny they were on their way, but I wasn't going to help them catch him. I was his mother and despite everything I didn't want to see him arrested and jailed for life.

EPILOGUE

I haven't seen Danny since that afternoon in the bar in St Lucia. By the time the police arrived, we'd all agreed to tell them we didn't know where Danny was and neither did we know anything about any drugs on board *Duchess*. The police came to the conclusion themselves that Erin was looking for revenge and therefore likely lying after no trace was found on *Duchess*.

With the delay in handing *Duchess* over to her owners, and Danny disappearing I never did have enough money to pay Big Malky, so it was only a matter of time before he caught up with me. He sent two of his goons round to 'teach me a lesson' and leave the message he still expected his money.

I have to keep reminding myself it wasn't all for nothing, though. Danny might not have come through for me, but he was still *alive*. I'd done what any good mother would; *whatever* it took to protect my child.

Danny's message had been waiting for me when we arrived in Gran Canaria and my phone signal reconnected. He was in over his head and there was nowhere else for him to turn. I didn't know what to do at first, but then an opportunity presented itself and I took it before I had a chance to think it through.

I'd gone for a walk round the marina to try to clear my head after drinking too much. I had no idea Erin was out too and my first thought when I saw her push Hugo down the stairs was to go and help them. Had Hugo come on to Erin again?

And then, as I stood in the shadows watching Erin hurrying away, the devil whispered in my drunken ear.

If he can't sail, then Danny could take his place.

I shrugged that devil off, a shiver running through me. What kind of person wished injury on someone they considered a friend?

But you could help yourself and *Danny.*

Hugo tried to stand up, half-drunk, half-dazed from the fall. Before I had the time to understand what I was doing, I picked up a discarded belaying pin, strode forward and struck him hard on the head – twice. (I hid the belaying pin in one of the cockpit lockers and disposed of it during a night watch when no one was looking.)

I wasn't trying to kill Hugo, just make sure he wasn't well enough to sail with us. A concussion, that's all that was needed. It meant I could justify inviting Danny, and the drugs, on board. Win-win.

When I realised how badly I'd injured Hugo, I was devastated, but it was too late. I couldn't change what I'd done. I couldn't help Hugo, but I could help Danny. I ignored that it was my fault Hugo was in hospital, shoved it into a dark corner of my mind and left it there, choosing instead to focus on the tasks at hand.

I was paying for it now, of course. The guilt was crippling at times, but I had no option other than to work through it. It wasn't as though I could ask my therapist for coping mechanisms.

The last thing I'd been expecting to hear from Erin was that Danny was somehow involved in Rhea's death. I held her hand both literally and metaphorically for months and if I had one question for her, it would be to ask why she didn't tell me. I would've believed her without question back then.

Daylight was beginning to seep through the window, and I decided it was late enough to have avoided Nurse Beelzebub. I was so uncomfortable, I no longer cared if it was her who responded to my call.

As I reached for my buzzer, the ward door swished open hesitantly. I peered at the silhouette framed in the open doorway.

'Nurse?'

'Mum?'

'Danny?' I'd know that voice anywhere. 'What are you doing here?'

'I need your help, Mum.'

THE END

AUTHOR'S NOTE

If, like Helen, you or someone you love is struggling with debt or gambling addiction, don't suffer in silence, help is available.

Gambling Addiction Help and Advice

https://www.begambleaware.org/how-help-loved-one-who-gambles

https://www.gamcare.org.uk/

Help with Debt

https://www.citizensadvice.org.uk/debt-and-money/help-with-debt/

https://www.stepchange.org/how-we-help/debt-advice.aspx

ACKNOWLEDGEMENTS

I find myself utterly amazed that it's time to write the acknowledgements for my *third* book! And yet, somehow, this does not get any easier and the fear of forgetting someone grows ever greater.

First and foremost, I'd like to thank my publisher, Bloodhound Books. Betsy, Fred, Tara, Kate, Vicky and Abbie, you have always had my back and I know more than most the work that goes into getting a book out there. Thank you for all your hard work.

Thanks go to my editor, Clare, who got what I was trying to achieve straight away and worked solidly to help me get it there; my proofreader, Ian; and my beta-reader, Maria. You guys rock!

Betsy – as ever, woman, your advice was spot on – even if it did mean me having to rewrite half the book! It was totally worth it; thank you for helping me wrestle *The Boat Trip* into shape.

HUGE thanks *have* to go to all the readers, bloggers, book reviewers and anyone who shares bookish content. None of us writers would be able to do what we do if it weren't for you.

Massive thanks, as always, to Jen Faulkner. This woman has had my back whenever I've doubted myself, has read virtually every word I have ever written and never fails to support and encourage me. However, she is now banned from making dinner reservations. (If you want to know the full story, buy me a drink and I'll tell you all about it!)

I couldn't have written this book without the specific help of Joe Johnson, Lorraine Stevens and Kate Cope. All of whom gave me expert advice on sailing yachts, crossing the Atlantic, what it's like to be stuck on a boat for weeks at a time and generally answered all of my inane questions. Any mistakes that remain are mine and mine alone.

My non-bookish friends have never wavered in their support and enthusiasm from *Open Your Eyes* to this one. Joe, Di, Steve, Bev, Mike, Polly, Heather, Norman, El, Kezia, Beckie and Janice – thank you!

If you know me, then you know I love a book festival, and these guys help to make them the incredible weekends they always are: Anne, Mik, the two Robs, Danny, Effie, Jen, Howard, Debbie, Norman, Lesley, Jack, Lauren, Libby, Sam, Antony, Louise and Abir – thank you for your friendship! (If I've forgotten you – sorry, clearly I spent too much time at the bar with you!)

My family have been so incredibly supportive I can hardly believe it. Mum, Dad, Pamela, Craig, Lily, Teddy, Ivy and Henry, I love you all. Thank you for making all of *this* feel so special.

As ever, my final word goes to my husband, Stuart. His encouragement, support and constant reminders of how well I'm doing lift me when things are tough and make me grin like a mad woman when things are going well. Although I get better at telling people I'm a writer all the time, he's still always the first to find my books on Amazon and show anyone who shows even the smallest amount of interest. I don't think it's hyperbole to say, I couldn't do this without you, honey – THANK YOU!

ALSO BY HEATHER J. FITT

Open Your Eyes

———

The Flight

A NOTE FROM THE PUBLISHER

Thank you for reading this book. If you enjoyed it please do consider leaving a review on Amazon to help others find it too.

We hate typos. All of our books have been rigorously edited and proofread, but sometimes mistakes do slip through. If you have spotted a typo, please do let us know and we can get it amended within hours.

info@bloodhoundbooks.com

Made in the USA
Monee, IL
22 August 2023

41440911R00152